U0020835

+ 挑戰級

GEPT 全民英檢初級

單字加碼記憶法

利用已經認識的字，輕易記住更多單字！

英文形似字「加碼式」聯想記憶法

吳惠珠 著

作者序

作者序

坊間的英文單字書已充斥著按字母序、出現頻率、字源、詞類、同義字、反義字、主題、分類、隨機、逆向等不同方式編排的書，而拙作《舉一反三記單字》是以列舉單字的名詞、動詞、形容詞、副詞來「一次學個夠」，《TOEIC單字得來速》則是以分析單字的字首、字根、字尾來「各個擊破」，在上述這兩本書推出之後，有讀者來向我反映，他們覺得有些字是無法利用詞類、字根概念來拆解的，也因為有這些寶貴的意見，觸動我的靈感，我決定使用詞類、字源以外的方法，讓讀者以「形似字聯想法」來一勞永逸地記住單字。

weight（體重）、flight（班機）、knight（騎士）、fright（驚嚇）這四個字看起來不太好記，如果換個方式，先寫出eight（八），再加上w，weight這個字就可輕易記住，而且絕對不會拼錯。以此類推，light（燈）加上f變成flight，night（夜）加上k變成knight，right加上f變成fright，利用這種「加碼」方式，保證可以讓你成為拼字高手！

再看看metal（金屬）、mental（精神的）、moral（寓意）、morale（士氣）這四個長得很像的字，如果用「加碼式」記憶法，metal加個n變成mental，moral加個e變成morale，是不是頓時間覺得好記多了？

「加碼式」的記憶法也可以反轉過來用，例如，patent（專利）這個字看起來似乎不好記，但是，只要已學過patient（病人；有耐心的）這個字，把中間的i去掉，就可以輕易記住patent了。還有，把window（窗）這個字的n去掉，就可以輕易記住widow（寡婦）這個字。

「加碼式」記憶法就是要讓讀者利用已經認識的字，輕易記住更多單字！本書分成21章，每一章整理出加上a、b、c、d、e、f、g、h、i、l、m、n、o、p、r、s、t、u、w、y等不同字母後，就可以成為另一個字的組合。這種把長得像的字分組，一次只記兩個字，是無負擔、最輕鬆、有效的背單字方法。此外，為了要讓各位讀者按各人不同程度、不同需求來記住單字，我把單字分成兩個級數，「實用級」中所收錄的字較短、較實用，「挑戰級」中所收錄的字，「顧名思義」稍具挑戰性，是較長的單字，但是，各位讀者不必恐懼，只要有耐心地用本書裡所整理出來的方法記單字，相信一定可以輕易記住，而且日後要再回想起來也不難。

前幾天看到一則笑話，有位老先生走進某家連鎖的美語補習班，櫃台小姐問老先生是不是要來幫孩子報名，老先生回答是要替自己報名。原來是老先生的兒子去美國留學，認識了美籍女朋友，現在結了婚，要回台灣定居，老先生希望可以和這位洋媳婦交流溝通，所以想來學英文。櫃台小姐問老先生：「您今年幾歲呀？」「68！」櫃台小姐又對老先生說：「要聽懂、會講英語至少也要學個兩年，那時您都70歲了耶。」老先生反問櫃台小姐：「小姐，難道我現在不學英文，兩年後會是66歲嗎？」

我想用 Better late than never. 這句話送給因這本書而結緣的讀者，在英文學習路上你或許遲了些才加入，但總比從沒開始試過來得好，只要開始，永不嫌遲！

「加碼式」記憶法是個創新的學習方式，希望這個「史上第一」的新學習法讓你的英文學習路一路順暢。在英文的學習路上，英文單字的識字量永遠不嫌多，請各位讀者以這本書做為一個開始，奠定了單字基礎後，更能徜徉於閱讀英文原文書的樂趣中。

作者　吳惠珠

吳惠珠

民國96年暑假

目錄

如何使用本書

《單字加碼記憶法》目的在於加強字彙能力、訓練發音拼字，適合一般程度成人自修，並可做為國中、小英文老師補充教材。

使用本書時，建議與MP3光碟合併使用，以收最佳訓練效果。

步驟 1 本書以「形似字彙」並列編輯而成，讀者開始閱讀各章之前，可先利用「試試看」頁面自我測試，看看是否認得加入「加碼字母」前後的字。

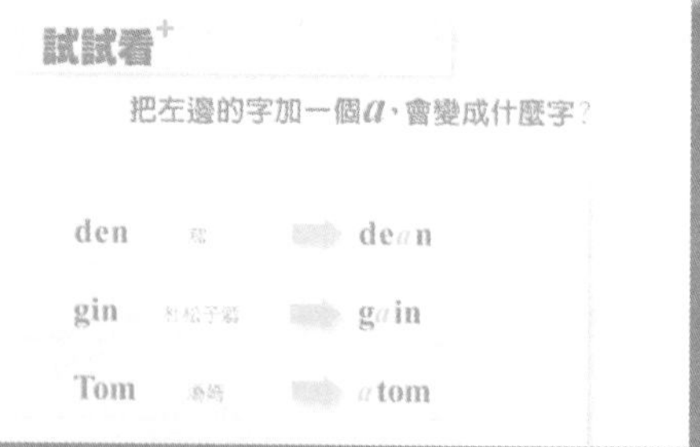

試試看
把左邊的字加一個a，會變成什麼字?
den → dean
gin → gain
Tom → atom

步驟 2 左頁為「加碼前字彙」，右頁為「加碼後字彙」
聆聽MP3朗讀，仔細比較左邊字彙加上一個字母之後，發音產生何種變化光筆使用者可點選喇叭圖案，進行單句跟讀。
★光筆購買、使用相關問題，歡迎洽詢本公司客服專線：02-2708-5875，
客服信箱：service@heliopolis.com.tw

MP3-201

den The rabbits live in a small den by the barn.

gin He likes a glass of gin after dinner.

Tom Why can't I hang out with Tom?

dean This applica... dean.

gain She gained a... honest.

atom Water is mad...

步驟

為幫助讀者測試學習成果，避免囫圇吞棗，本書各章均附兩種測驗：「想想看（填空）」及「找找看（改錯）」。
「想想看」要在指定的八個字當中，找出符合句義的字。
「找找看」要在各章已出現過的例句當中，找出拼寫錯誤的地方。

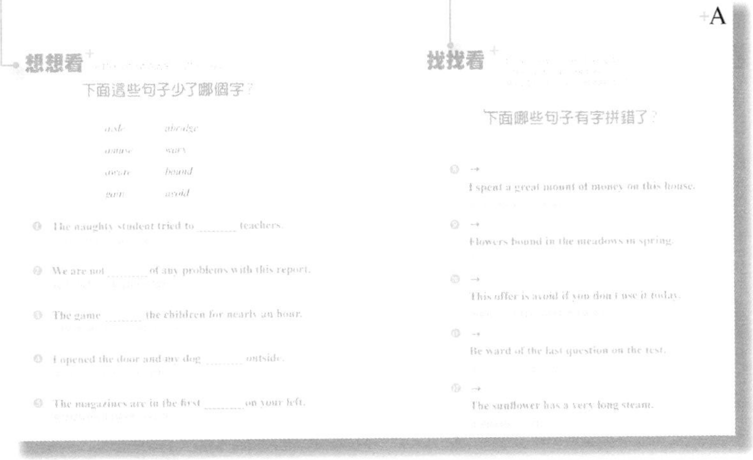

A

想想看

下面這些句子少了哪個字？

aisle *abridge*
amuse *wary*
aware *bound*
gain *avoid*

1. The naughty student tried to ________ teachers.
2. We are not ________ of any problems with this report.
3. The game ________ the children for nearly an hour.
4. I opened the door and my dog ________ outside.
5. The magazines are in the first ________ on your left.

找找看

下面哪些句子有字拼錯了？

1. → I spent a great mount of money on this house.
2. → Flowers bound in the meadows in spring.
3. → This offer is avoid if you don't use it today.
4. → Be ward of the last question on the test.
5. → The sunflower has a very long steam.

步驟

各章測驗解答位於各章最後一頁。

加碼字母 +A

試試看

把左邊的字加一個*a*，會變成什麼字？

den	窩	**de*a*n**	
gin	杜松子酒	**g*a*in**	
Tom	湯姆	***a*tom**	
wry	扭曲的	**w*a*ry**	
isle	小島	***a*isle**	
muse	沈思	***a*muse**	
stem	莖	**ste*a*m**	
void	空的	***a*void**	

試試看

把右邊的字減一個*a*，會變成什麼字？

ward	→	***a*ward** 獎
ware	→	***a*ware** 知道的
bound	→	***a*bound** 充滿
mount	→	***a*mount** 數量
spire	→	***a*spire** 渴望
bridge	→	***a*bridge** 刪節
scribe	→	***a*scribe** 歸因於…
vocation	→	***a*vocation** 副業

MP3-201

den
[dɛn]
名 窩

The rabbits live in a small den by the barn.
那些兔子住在穀倉旁的小窩裡。

gin
[dʒɪn]
名 杜松子酒

He likes a glass of gin after dinner.
他喜歡在晚餐後喝杯杜松子酒。

Tom
[tɑm]
名 湯姆

Why can't I hang out with Tom?
為什麼我不能跟湯姆出去玩?

wry
[raɪ]
形 扭曲的

He gave us the news with a wry smile.
他帶著扭曲的微笑告訴我們那個消息。

isle
[aɪl]
名 小島

There are several small isles around the main island.
主島附近有好幾座小島。

muse
[mjuz]
動 沈思

She mused that the plan would likely fail.
她暗自想著那個計畫可能會失敗。

stem
[stɛm]
名 莖

The sunflower has a very long stem.
向日葵的莖很長。

void
[vɔɪd]
形 無效的

This offer is void if you don't use it today.
如果你今天不用,這個提供條件就無效了。

dean
[din]
名 學院院長

This application must be sent directly to the dean.
這張申請表必須直接寄給院長。

gain
[gen]
動 得到

She gained a reputation for being kind and honest.
她的善良正直有口皆碑。

atom
[`ætəm]
名 原子

Water is made of two kinds of atoms.
水是由兩種原子組成。

wary
[`wɛrɪ]
形 小心翼翼的

Be wary of the last question on the test.
要小心考卷上的最後一個問題。

aisle
[aɪl]
名 走道

The vegetables are in the aisle on the right side of the store.
蔬菜擺在商店右邊的走道上。

amuse
[ə`mjuz]
動 給…提供娛樂

They were amused by the jokes he told.
他們被他說的笑話逗得很開心。

steam
[stim]
名 蒸汽

They saw the steam coming from the pot of water.
他們看到蒸汽從那鍋水中冒出來。

avoid
[ə`vɔɪd]
動 避免

Please avoid making spelling mistakes on your paper.
你的報告上請避免拼字錯誤。

MP3-202

ward
[wɔrd]
名 病房

This hospital has constructed a new cancer ward.
這家醫院已建置了一間新的癌症病房。

ware
[wɛr]
名 商品

He brought his wares to try to sell.
他帶來他的商品試圖販售。

bound
[baʊnd]
動 跳躍

The dog bounded out the door as soon as it saw the cat outside.
狗一看到外頭的貓就跳出門外。

mount
[maʊnt]
動 爬上

The policeman mounted the horse and chased after the robber.
警察攀爬馬背去追捕強盜。

spire
[spaɪr]
動 尖塔

There is a spire on top of this church.
這間教堂上方有一座尖塔。

bridge
[brɪdʒ]
名 橋

The bridge is falling apart because of the heavy rain.
因為豪雨，這座橋已經快垮了。

scribe
[skraɪb]
名 抄寫員

The king had his scribe write the letter.
國王要他的抄寫員寫那封信。

vocation
[voˋkeʃən]
名 職業

He chose his vocation based on his father's advice.
他依照他父親的建議選擇職業。

award
[ə`wɔrd]
動 授予，給予

The company awarded him with a free ticket to New York.
公司送他一張去紐約的免費機票作為獎勵。

aware
[ə`wɛr]
形 知道的

I am aware that this is a difficult job.
我知道這是一個困難的工作。

abound
[ə`baʊnd]
動 充滿

Flowers abound in the meadows in spring.
春天時這片草原充滿了花朵。

amount
[ə`maʊnt]
名 數量

I spent a great amount of money on this house.
我為這個房子花了一大筆錢。

aspire
[ə`spaɪr]
動 嚮往

I really aspire to the research atmosphere of good schools overseas.
我非常嚮往國外名校的研究風氣。

abridge
[ə`brɪdʒ]
動 刪節

This abridged book is cheaper and lighter than the original.
這本刪節本比原版便宜、輕巧。

ascribe
[ə`skraɪb]
動 把…歸因(於)

This delivery problem was ascribed to a manufacturing problem in the factory.
交貨的問題歸因於工廠製造時的缺失。

avocation
[ævə`keʃən]
名 副業

He spends too much time on his avocations.
他花太多時間在副業上。

想想看 要將填入的字改為合乎文法的形式喔！

下面這些句子少了哪個字？

aisle	*abridge*
amuse	*wary*
aware	*bound*
gain	*avoid*

1. **The naughty student tried to _______ teachers.**
   這個頑皮學生試圖躲避老師。

2. **We are not _______ of any problems with this report.**
   我們不知道這份報告有任何問題。

3. **The game _______ the children for nearly an hour.**
   這個遊戲讓孩子們開心地玩了快一個小時。

4. **I opened the door and my dog _______ outside.**
   我一打開門，我的狗就跳了出來。

5. **The magazines are in the first _______ on your left.**
   雜誌都放在左手邊的第一個走道。

6. **Sally _______ five pounds in a week.**
   莎莉一星期內胖了五鎊。

7. **This book has been _______ to 100 pages.**
   這本書被刪節到剩下一百頁。

找找看

以下句子在前面都出現過，你確定都讀熟了嗎？
找找看下面的句子有沒有拼錯的字。
錯字訂正於上方箭頭處，沒錯字請打“○”

下面哪些句子有字拼錯了？

8 →

I spent a great mount of money on this house.

我為這個房子花了一大筆錢。

9 →

Flowers bound in the meadows in spring.

春天時這片草原充滿了花朵。

10 →

This offer is avoid if you don't use it today.

如果你今天不用，這個提供條件就無效了。

11 →

Be ward of the last question on the test.

要小心考卷上的最後一個問題。

12 →

The sunflower has a very long steam.

那朵向日葵的莖很長。

13 →

Please void making spelling mistakes on your paper.

你的報告上請避免拼字錯誤。

❶ avoid
❷ aware
❸ amused
❹ bounded
❺ aisle
❻ gained
❼ abridged
❽ mount → amount
❾ bound → abound
❿ avoid → void
⓫ ward → wary
⓬ steam → stem
⓭ void → avoid

>>>測驗解答

加碼字母

+B

試試看

把左邊的字加一個*b*，會變成什麼字？

so	如此	→	**so*b***
ark	方舟	→	***b*ark**
her	她的	→	**her*b***
owl	貓頭鷹	→	***b*owl**
rag	破布	→	***b*rag**
Tom	湯姆（人名）	→	**tom*b***
itch	癢	→	***b*itch**
lame	跛腳的	→	***b*lame**

試試看

把右邊的字減一個*b*，會變成什麼字？

lush	→	***b*lush** 臉紅
race	→	***b*race** 牙齒矯正器
raid	→	***b*raid** 編成辮子
rake	→	***b*rake** 煞車
rush	→	***b*rush** 刷子
order	→	***b*order** 邊界
ounce	→	***b*ounce** 彈起
ranch	→	***b*ranch** 樹枝

MP3-203

so

[so]

副 如此，很

He came to my party so late.

他很晚才來我的派對。

ark

[ɑrk]

名 方舟

There's a famous story about an ark in this old book.

這本古書中有個關於方舟的著名故事。

her

[hɝ]

代 她的

Patience is her first attribute.

有耐心是她最大的特質。

owl

[aʊl]

名 貓頭鷹

The owl sat in a tree looking for mice.

貓頭鷹停在樹上尋找老鼠。

rag

[ræg]

名 破布

We used some rags to wipe up the oil on the ground.

我們用破布把地上的油擦起來。

Tom

[tɑm]

名 湯姆（人名）

Tom has a background in economics.

湯姆有經濟學的背景。

itch

[ɪtʃ]

名 癢

I have an itch on my arm where the mosquito bit me.

我的手臂被蚊子咬的地方在癢。

lame

[lem]

形 跛腳的

The man's leg is lame from an old injury.

那個男子的腿因舊傷不良於行。

sob
[sɑb]
動 啜泣

The girl sobbed alone in the dark.
那個女孩獨自在黑暗中啜泣。

bark
[bɑrk]
動 吠叫

Her dog only barks at me so I don't think he likes me.
她的狗只對著我叫，所以我不覺得牠喜歡我。

herb
[ɝb]
名 草本植物

I've started taking some herbs for my high blood pressure.
我已經開始食用一些藥草來控制我的高血壓。

bowl
[bol]
動 滾

He pushed the rock and watched it bowl down the hill.
他推了那塊石頭，並看著它滾下山去。

brag
[bræg]
動 自誇

I just hope he doesn't start bragging again!
希望他別又開始吹牛了！

tomb
[tum]
名 墓

Thieves sometimes uncover ancient tombs to steal jewelry.
竊賊有時會挖開古墓偷珠寶。

bitch
[bɪtʃ]
名 母狗

This bitch has a new litter of puppies.
母狗生了一窩小狗。

blame
[blem]
動 責備

I was blamed for not calling the boss about the problem.
我因為沒打電話向老闆報告這個問題而被責備。

MP3-204

lush

[lʌʃ]

形 蒼翠繁茂的

The lush field is filled with plants and flowers.

這片茂盛的田野長滿了植物和花朵。

race

[res]

名 比賽

The athletes got ready to run in the race.

那個運動員已經準備好要賽跑了。

raid

[red]

動 襲擊

The village was raided just after dark.

那座村莊天一黑就遭到襲擊。

rake

[rek]

名 耙子

Use this rake to clean the yard.

拿這支耙子去清理院子。

rush

[rʌʃ]

動 匆促行事

He rushed into the classroom twenty minutes late.

他衝進教室時遲到了二十分鐘。

order

[`ɔrdɚ]

動 點菜

She ordered French fries and a hamburger.

她點了薯條和漢堡。

ounce

[aʊns]

名 盎司

They use ounces to weigh things in the United States.

美國用盎司當秤重單位。

ranch

[ræntʃ]

名 農場

We have to go to a ranch if we want to ride some horses.

我們如果想要騎馬，就得去牧場。

blush
[blʌʃ]
動 臉紅

He blushed when he knew he made a stupid mistake.
得知自己犯了個愚蠢的錯誤時，他臉紅了。

brace
[bres]
名 牙齒矯正器

My sister wore braces to have her teeth fixed.
我妹妹戴牙套矯正牙齒。

braid
[bred]
動 編成辮子

I'd like my hair braided.
我想要把頭髮編成辮子。

brake
[brek]
動 煞車

Don't brake while turning.
轉彎時不要踩煞車。

brush
[brʌʃ]
名 刷子

He used an old brush to clean his shoes.
他用一把舊刷子清理他的鞋子。

border
[`bɔrdɚ]
名 邊界

There is a conflict at the border of the two countries.
在這兩國邊境有一場衝突。

bounce
[bauns]
動 彈起

The ball fell off the shelf and bounced away.
球從架子上掉下來又彈走了。

branch
[bræntʃ]
名 樹枝

The branches on the tree broke under the weight of the snow.
那棵樹的枝幹因為雪的重量而折斷了。

想想看 要將填入的字改為合乎文法的形式喔！

下面這些句子少了哪個字？

brush	*sob*
rag	*brag*
blame	*tomb*
bark	*order*

❶ **That dog _______ loudly, but it is friendly.**
那隻狗叫得很大聲，不過其實牠很溫馴。

❷ **She _______ her hair after taking a shower.**
她淋浴之後梳了梳頭髮。

❸ **She _______ for over an hour when her cat died.**
她的貓死掉時，她哭了一個多鐘頭。

❹ **Don't _______ me for your mistakes!**
不要把你的錯怪到我頭上來！

❺ **The waiter asked if we were ready to _______.**
服務生問我們是否可以點餐了。

❻ **He likes to _______ about how fast he drives.**
他喜歡吹噓自己開車飛快的速度。

❼ **You can use this _______ to wash your car.**
你可以用這塊破布來洗車。

找找看

以下句子在前面都出現過，你確定都讀熟了嗎？
找找看下面的句子有沒有拼錯的字。
錯字訂正於上方箭頭處，沒錯字請打"○"

下面哪些句子有字拼錯了？

8 → ____________

He used an old blush to clean his shoes.

他用一把舊刷子清理他的鞋子。

9 → ____________

The girl sobed alone in the dark.

那個女孩獨自在黑暗中啜泣。

10 → ____________

The rush field is filled with plants and flowers.

這片茂盛的田野長滿了植物和花朵。

11 → ____________

I just hope he doesn't start ragging again!

希望他別又開始吹牛了！

12 → ____________

I'd like my hair braided.

我想要把頭髮編成辮子。

13 → ____________

We have to go to a branch if we want to ride some horses.

我們如果想要騎馬，就要去牧場。

1. barks
2. brushed
3. sobbed
4. blame
5. order
6. brag
7. rag
8. blush → brush
9. sobed → sobbed
10. rush → lush
11. ragging → bragging
12. ○
13. branch → ranch

>>>測驗解答

加碼字母 +C

試試看

把左邊的字加一個*c*，會變成什麼字？

aid	幫助	→	**a*c*id**
hop	跳躍	→	***c*hop**
one	一個	→	***c*one**
ram	公羊	→	***c*ram**
ease	減輕	→	***c*ease**
fore	前部	→	**for*c*e**
harm	損害	→	***c*harm**
hart	雄鹿	→	***c*hart**

試試看

把右邊的字減一個*c*，會變成什麼字？

lash	→	*c*lash 衝突
lone	→	*c*lone 複製品
oral	→	*c*oral 珊瑚
raft	→	*c*raft 工藝
rude	→	*c*rude 未成熟的
leave	→	*c*leave 劈開
ripple	→	*c*ripple 跛子
sandal	→	s*c*andal 醜聞

MP3-205

aid
[ed]
動 幫助

We should aid those who are less fortunate than us.
我們應該幫助那些比我們不幸的人。

hop
[hap]
動 跳躍，齊足跳

The rabbit hopped away into the forest.
兔子跳進森林裡了。

one
[wʌn]
代 一個

One of the cars we own will be sold tomorrow.
我們有一部車明天會賣出去。

ram
[ræm]
名 公羊

The ram ran up the side of the mountain.
公羊跑到山坡上。

ease
[iz]
動 減輕

The young lady took some pills to ease her headache.
那位小姐吃了一些藥丸來舒緩頭痛。

fore
[for]
名 前部

He spoke their names and they came to the fore.
他叫他們的名字，他們就到前面來。

harm
[harm]
名 損害

Cigarettes will do you harm.
香菸會危害你的健康。

hart
[hart]
名 雄鹿

The student was asked to explain what a hart is.
學生被要求解釋什麼是雄鹿。

acid
[ˋæsɪd]
形 酸的

The acid rain damages the soil.
酸雨破壞土壤。

chop
[tʃɑp]
動 砍，切

Mom is chopping vegetables.
媽媽正在切菜。

cone
[kon]
名 圓錐

She made a hat shaped like a cone.
她做了一頂圓錐型的帽子。

cram
[kræm]
動 把…塞進

He crammed the last of his things into his car.
他把他最後的一樣東西塞進車裡。

cease
[sis]
動 停止

The two armies ceased fighting and decided to talk about peace.
兩軍停火，決定進行和平對談。

force
[fors]
動 強迫

He was forced to admit his mistake.
他被迫承認錯誤。

charm
[tʃɑrm]
名 魅力

The charm of the lady attracts everyone's eye.
這位女士的魅力吸引了大家的目光。

chart
[tʃɑrt]
名 圖表

The doctor looked at the patient's chart.
醫生看了病人的病歷。

MP3-206

lash
[læʃ]
動 鞭打

The cruel man lashed the old horse repeatedly.
狠心的男人不斷鞭打那匹老馬。

lone
[lon]
形 孤單的

The lone wolf stood atop the mountain.
那匹孤狼站在山頂上。

oral
[`orəl]
形 口頭的

We have an oral exam this morning.
我們今天早上有一場口試。

raft
[ræft]
名 木筏

The kids built a small raft to use on the lake.
孩子們造了一個小木筏在湖裡划。

rude
[rud]
形 粗野的

It's rude to talk when you are eating.
邊吃東西邊講話很沒禮貌。

leave
[liv]
動 離開

I'll leave the house after I'm done eating.
我吃完之後會離開這間房子。

ripple
[`rɪpl]
名 漣漪

The fish made ripples on the water's surface.
魚在水面激起了漣漪。

sandal
[`sændl]
名 涼鞋

You should not wear sandals when going to see a play.
去觀賞舞台劇時不應該穿涼鞋。

clash
[klæʃ]
動 衝突

The two armies clashed by the river.
兩支軍隊在河邊起了衝突。

clone
[klon]
名 複製品

This CD is a clone of the one you gave me.
這張CD是你給我那張的複製品。

coral
[ˋkɔrəl]
名 珊瑚

They swam in the ocean and looked at the coral and fish.
他們在海裡游泳，觀賞珊瑚和魚類。

craft
[kræft]
名 工藝

Paula's favorite class was always arts and crafts.
寶拉最喜歡的課一直是美術及工藝。

crude
[krud]
形 未成熟的

She showed us a crude drawing of her home.
她給我們看她家的草圖。

cleave
[kliv]
動 劈開

The heavy knife easily cleaved the meat.
那把大刀輕易地就把肉切開了。

cripple
[ˋkrɪpl̩]
名 跛子

This cripple has many friends.
這個跛子有很多朋友。

scandal
[ˋskændl̩]
名 醜聞

It's well known that Bill Clinton was involved in several scandals.
柯林頓總統涉及多起醜聞的事眾所皆知。

想想看 要將填入的字改為合乎文法的形式喔！

下面這些句子少了哪個字？

acid	*chart*
hop	*chop*
harm	*scandal*
cram	*aid*

1. **Smoking is known to _______ people's health.**
大家都知道吸菸對健康有害。

2. **The _______ rain is caused by pollution.**
酸雨是由污染造成的。

3. **He _______ the last suitcase into his small car.**
他把最後一個行李箱塞進他那輛小車裡。

4. **The rabbit _______ into the forest when it saw the dogs.**
一見到狗，兔子就跳進森林裡。

5. **This _______ shows the average temperature in New York for each month.**
這張圖表顯示紐約每個月的平均溫度。

6. **The old woman wears a hearing _______.**
老婦人戴了一副助聽器。

7. **It seems that the media is most interested in covering political _______.**
媒體似乎最有興趣報導政治醜聞。

以下句子在前面都出現過，你確定都讀熟了嗎？
找找看下面的句子有沒有拼錯的字。
錯字訂正於上方箭頭處，沒錯字請打"○"

下面哪些句子有字拼錯了？

❽ →

Paula's favorite class was always arts and rafts.

寶拉最喜歡的課始終是美術及工藝。

❾ →

This cripple has many friends.

這個跛子有很多朋友。

❿ →

The young lady took some pills to cease her headache.

那位小姐吃了一些藥丸來舒緩頭痛。

⓫ →

You should not wear scandals when going to see a play.

去觀賞舞台劇時不應該穿涼鞋。

⓬ →

He was fored to admit his mistake.

他被迫承認錯誤。

⓭ →

He cram the last of his things into his car.

他把他的最後一樣東西塞進車裡。

1. harm
2. acid
3. crammed
4. hopped
5. chart
6. aid
7. scandals
8. rafts → crafts
9. ○
10. cease → ease
11. scandals → sandals
12. fored → forced
13. cram → crammed

>>>測驗解答

加碼字母 +D

試試看

把左邊的字加一個*d*，會變成什麼字？

art	藝術	→	***d*art**	
ash	灰燼	→	***d*ash**	
her	她的	→	**her*d***	
rug	小地毯	→	***d*rug**	
rum	蘭姆酒	→	***d*rum**	
she	她	→	**she*d***	
war	戰爭	→	**war*d***	
woo	求愛	→	**woo*d***	

試試看

把右邊的字減一個*d*，會變成什麼字？

aunt	→	***d*aunt** 嚇
boar	→	**boar*d*** 布告欄
itch	→	***d*itch** 溝
plea	→	**plea*d*** 懇求
raft	→	***d*raft** 草稿
read	→	***d*read** 懼怕
rift	→	***d*rift** 漂流
shrew	→	**shrew*d*** 精明的

MP3-207

art
[ɑrt]
名 藝術

She studies art at the new university.
她在那所新的大學研讀藝術。

ash
[æʃ]
名 灰燼

The house was burnt to ashes.
這棟房子被燒成灰燼。

her
[hɜ]
代 她的

Her name is Samantha but her friends all call her Sam.
她的名字叫莎曼莎，可是她的朋友都叫她珊。

rug
[rʌg]
名 小地毯

She put a rug in her living room.
她在客廳裡放了一塊小地毯。

rum
[rʌm]
名 蘭姆酒

Rum is a popular drink in Hawaii.
萊姆酒在夏威夷是一種受歡迎的飲品。

she
[ʃi]
代 她

She listens to the broadcast every Sunday night.
她每個星期天晚上都聽廣播節目。

war
[wɔr]
名 戰爭

The Second World War went on for four years.
第二次世界大戰持續了四年。

woo
[wu]
動 求愛

John tried to woo Jessica to date him, but she wasn't interested in him.
約翰試圖找潔西卡約會，可是她對他沒興趣。

dart
[dɑrt]
動 狂奔

The mouse darted out of the hole in the ground.
老鼠從地上的洞竄出。

dash
[dæʃ]
名 猛衝

He dashed into the room and put out the fire.
他衝進房間把火撲滅。

herd
[hɜd]
動 畜群

There's a herd of sheep standing in the field.
有一群綿羊站在草原上。

drug
[drʌg]
名 藥品，毒品

Stay away from drugs.
遠離毒品。

drum
[drʌm]
名 鼓

My brother plays the drums in a rock band.
我哥哥在搖滾樂團裡打鼓。

shed
[ʃɛd]
動 流出

She sheds tears every time she watches this movie.
她每次看這部電影都會流眼淚。

ward
[wɔrd]
動 擋開

They say this necklace will ward off evil spirits.
據說這條項鍊可以阻擋邪靈。

wood
[wud]
動 木頭

Please gather some wood to build a fire.
請找些木材生火。

MP3-208

aunt
[ænt]
名 阿姨，嬸嬸

I live with my aunt and uncle.
我和叔叔、嬸嬸住在一起。

boar
[bor]
名 公豬

Be careful of that boar.
小心那隻公豬。

itch
[ɪtʃ]
名 癢

The dog has an itch on its foot.
這隻狗的腳有個地方在癢。

plea
[pli]
名 懇求

He heard the children's pleas for their ball.
他聽見那些孩子在懇求要回他們的球。

raft
[ræft]
名 木筏

The raft was too small to take on the ocean.
木筏太小了，不能在大海上航行。

read
[rid]
動 讀

You must read this book and then write a paper about it.
你要先讀這本書，然後寫一篇相關報告。

rift
[rɪft]
名 裂縫

They noticed a rift in the land near the mountain.
他們發現了山邊地上的一條裂縫。

shrew
[ʃru]
名 潑婦

That poor man is married to an old shrew.
那個可憐的男人娶了一個老潑婦。

daunt
[dɔnt]
動 嚇倒

We were daunted by the difficult jobs ahead of us.
我們被眼前艱難的工作給嚇倒了。

board
[bord]
名 布告欄

There was a notice on the board that said we were getting a new teacher.
布告欄上有一張公告，說我們會換一位新老師。

ditch
[dɪtʃ]
名 溝

The ditch is full of trash.
這條水溝充滿垃圾。

plead
[plid]
動 懇求

He pleaded with the judge to not send him to jail.
他懇求法官不要把他關進牢裡。

draft
[dræft]
名 草稿

We need to see a rough draft of your project by Friday.
我們星期五之前需要看你對那個案子的大致構想。

dread
[drɛd]
動 懼怕

I dread this upcoming exam.
我很擔心即將到來的考試。

drift
[drɪft]
動 漂流

The coconut drifted on the ocean for many months.
那顆椰子在海上漂了好幾個月。

shrewd
[ʃrud]
形 精明的，聰穎的

He made a shrewd decision that saved us a lot of money.
他做了聰明的決定，替我們省了很多錢。

想想看 要將填入的字改為合乎文法的形式喔！

下面這些句子少了哪個字？

aid	*dread*
shed	*plead*
board	*war*
rift	*rug*

1. **Many people died in the Second World _______.**
許多人死於二次世界大戰。

2. **He _______ with the policeman to let him go.**
他哀求警察放他一馬。

3. **Most people really _______ speaking in front of large crowds.**
大多數人都很害怕在大庭廣眾之前演說。

4. **The water here all _______ to the east side of the mountain.**
這裡的水都流到山的東側。

5. **There is a pink _______ by the doorway.**
玄關有一塊粉紅色的小地毯。

6. **I know how to give first _______ in an emergency.**
我懂得如何進行緊急醫療急救。

7. **The farmer used a _______ to fix his barn.**
農夫用一塊板子修理穀倉。

找找看

以下句子在前面都出現過，你確定都讀熟了嗎？
找找看下面的句子有沒有拼錯的字。
錯字訂正於上方箭頭處，沒錯字請打“○”

下面哪些句子有字拼錯了？

8 →

They noticed a raft in the land near the mountain.

他們發現了山邊地上的一條裂縫。

9 →

He pleases with the judge to not send him to jail.

他懇求法官不要把他關進牢裡。

10 →

He ashed into the room and put out the fire.

他衝進房間把火撲滅。

11 →

She sheds tears every time she watches this movie.

她每次看這部電影都會流眼淚。

12 →

We were daunted by the difficult jobs ahead of us.

我們被眼前艱難的工作給嚇倒了。

13 →

He heard the children's plead for their ball.

他聽見那些孩子在懇求要回他們的球。

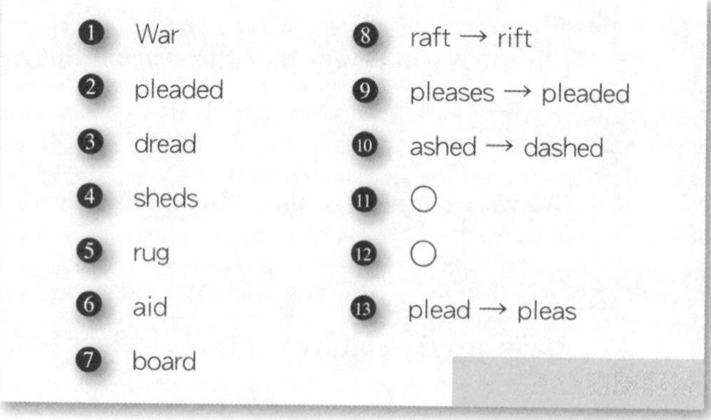

1. War
2. pleaded
3. dread
4. sheds
5. rug
6. aid
7. board
8. raft → rift
9. pleases → pleaded
10. ashed → dashed
11. ○
12. ○
13. plead → pleas

加碼字母 +E

試試看

把左邊的字加一個*e*，會變成什麼字？

go	去	***e*go**	
or	或者	**or*e***	
cap	帽子	**cap*e***	
dam	水壩	**dam*e***	
dim	昏暗的	**dim*e***	
fad	一時的流行	**fad*e***	
gap	間隔	**gap*e***	
mar	毀損	**mar*e***	

試試看

把右邊的字減一個*e*，會變成什麼字？

pop	→ **Pop*e***	教皇
rid	→ **rid*e***	騎
rip	→ **rip*e***	成熟的
rob	→ **rob*e***	袍子
tap	→ **tap*e***	膠帶
wag	→ **wag*e***	薪資
ally	→ **all*e*y**	小巷
bowl	→ **bow*e*l**	腸

試試看

把左邊的字加一個*e*，會變成什麼字？

gust	狂風	**gu*e*st**
past	超過	**past*e***
plat	地圖	**plat*e***
scar	疤	**scar*e***
sing	唱歌	**sing*e***
unit	單元，單位	**unit*e***
bacon	培根	**b*e*acon**
corps	兵團	**corps*e***

試試看

把右邊的字減一個*e*，會變成什麼字？

drive	→	**d*e*rive** 衍生
gorge	→	**G*e*orge** 喬治
haven	→	**h*e*aven** 天國
moral	→	**moral*e*** 士氣
strip	→	**strip*e*** 條紋
fright	→	**fr*e*ight** 運費
heroin	→	**heroin*e*** 女英雄
envelop	→	**envelop*e*** 信封

MP3-209

go
[go]
動 去

Do you want to go to the department store?
你想去百貨公司嗎？

or
[ɔr]
連 或者

I will visit the office on Wednesday or Thursday this week.
我會在這個星期的星期三或星期四拜訪貴公司。

cap
[kæp]
名 帽子

Teenagers like to wear baseball caps.
青少年喜歡戴棒球帽。

dam
[dæm]
名 水壩

The dam was made to help control the river.
建這個水壩是為了控制這條河的流量。

dim
[dɪm]
形 昏暗的

I can't see a thing in this dim light.
在這昏暗的燈光下，我什麼也看不到。

fad
[fæd]
名 一時的流行

Wearing a headband was a fad from the eighties.
戴頭巾是八〇年代的流行裝扮。

gap
[gæp]
名 間隔

Beware of the gap when you get on the MRT.
上捷運列車時，要當心月台間隙。

mar
[mɑr]
動 毀損

The performance was marred by a few small problems.
那場表演被一些小問題給毀了。

ego
[`igo]
名 自負，自我

Heather's got such a big ego because her father is so rich.
海瑟很自大，因為她爸爸很有錢。

ore
[or]
名 礦石

The land is valuable because it has a lot of iron ore.
這塊土地很有價值，因為含有很多鐵礦。

cape
[kep]
名 斗篷

If you put on this cape, you'll be warmer.
披上這件披肩，你會比較暖和。

dame
[dem]
名 女士

The dame said she comes from Camelot.
那位女士說她來自嘉美洛。

dime
[daɪm]
名 一角硬幣

A dime is a coin worth ten cents.
一角硬幣價值十分錢。

fade
[fed]
動 凋謝

The color faded away after washing.
顏色在洗過之後褪色變淡了。

gape
[gep]
動 目瞪口呆

They stood by and gaped at the scene of the accident.
他們站在一旁，被那場意外的景象嚇得目瞪口呆。

mare
[mɛr]
名 母馬

The farmer sold his best mare.
農夫賣掉了他最好的一匹母馬。

MP3-210

pop
[pɑp]
動 （突然）出現

A clown popped out of the present when I opened it.
我打開禮物時，一個小丑突然跳了出來。

rid
[rɪd]
動 免除

Matt is trying to get rid of his little brother.
麥特正在想辦法擺脫他弟弟。

rip
[rɪp]
動 撕

The newspaper ripped as he folded it.
他摺報紙時把它給撕破了。

rob
[rɑb]
動 搶劫

He was robbed last weekend.
他上週末被搶了。

tap
[tæp]
名 水龍頭

We called a man to fix the broken tap.
我們打電話叫人來修理壞掉的水龍頭。

wag
[wæg]
動 搖動

The dog wags its tail when it's happy or excited.
狗快樂或興奮時會搖尾巴。

ally
[ə`laɪ]
動 結盟

The war forced Italy to ally with Germany.
戰爭迫使義大利跟德國結盟。

bowl
[bol]
名 碗

I was so hungry that I had two bowls of rice.
我好餓，所以吃了兩碗飯。

Pope
[pop]
名 教皇

The Pope lives in the Vatican in Rome.
教宗住在羅馬的梵蒂岡。

ride
[raɪd]
動 騎

I'll ride my scooter to the library if it doesn't rain.
如果沒下雨，我會騎機車到圖書館去。

ripe
[raɪp]
形 成熟的

The farmer waits until the apples are all ripe before selling them.
農夫等到蘋果都熟了才將它們出售。

robe
[rob]
名 長袍

I like to wear a robe after I finish showering.
我喜歡沖完澡後穿上睡袍。

tape
[tep]
名 膠帶

We need some tapes to tighten up the chair.
我們需要一些膠帶來固定那張椅子。

wage
[wedʒ]
名 薪水

His new job only pays minimum wage.
他的新工作只付他最低薪資。

alley
[`ælɪ]
名 小巷

It's not safe to walk in alleys at midnight.
午夜時走小巷子並不安全。

bowel
[`bauəl]
名 腸

The doctor said he had a bowel problem.
醫生說他的腸子有問題。

MP3-211

gust
[gʌst]
名 一陣強風

A gust of wind blew the papers from the desk.
一陣強風吹落了書桌上的文件。

past
[pæst]
介 超過

It was past ten when we returned home.
我們回到家時超過十點了。

plat
[plæt]
名 地圖

He made a plat of the area.
他製作了一張這個地區的地圖。

scar
[skɑr]
名 疤

She has a small scar on her leg from a motorcycle accident.
她的腿上因為一場機車意外而留下一個小疤痕。

sing
[sɪŋ]
動 唱歌

The carolers went to every house singing Christmas carols.
耶誕頌歌隊到每一戶唱耶誕歌曲。

unit
[`junɪt]
名 單元

There are eleven units in each shipment.
每趟貨運會送出十一個單位的貨物。

bacon
[`bekən]
名 培根

Bacon fried with eggs is my favorite.
培根炒蛋是我的最愛。

corps
[kɔrps]
名 兵團

He learned to shoot while in the corps.
他入伍時學會射擊。

guest
[gɛst]
名 客人

We will have 50 guests tonight for my birthday party.
我今晚的生日派對將有五十個客人參加。

paste
[pest]
動 黏貼

Paste your drawings in the book, please.
請將你的畫貼在本子上。

plate
[plet]
名 盤子

She served the coffee along with a plate of cookies.
她端咖啡來時還附了一碟餅乾。

scare
[skɛr]
動 驚嚇

Sally is scared of dogs because she was bit once.
莎莉很怕狗，因為她曾經被狗咬過。

singe
[sɪndʒ]
動 燒焦

The edge of his shirt was singed in the fire.
他的襯衫邊緣在火災中燒焦了。

unite
[jʊ`naɪt]
動 聯合

We should unite and face our enemy together.
我們應該聯合起來一起面對敵人。

beacon
[`bikən]
名 燈塔

There is a beacon on top of the tall building.
那棟高樓頂端有一座燈塔。

corpse
[kɔrps]
名 屍體

Cryonics seeks to preserve corpses for resuscitation at a later date.
人體冷藏法是為了保存屍體以求日後復生。

MP3-212

drive
[draɪv]
動 開車

We'll drive to the factory tomorrow morning.
明天早上我們會開車去工廠。

gorge
[gɔrdʒ]
動 吞吃

They gorged themselves on fresh fruit.
他們飽嚐新鮮水果。

haven
[`hevən]
名 避難所

This building is a haven for stray dogs.
這棟建築物是流浪狗的避難所。

moral
[`mɔrəl]
名 寓意

"Do not lie" is a common moral in many stories.
「不要說謊」是許多故事中常見的寓意。

strip
[strɪp]
動 剝去

My brother stripped off his clothes and jumped into the pool.
我哥哥脫光衣服跳進池子。

fright
[fraɪt]
名 驚嚇

Her decision was poor because it was made in fright.
她的決定很不明智，因為是在倉皇中所做的。

heroin
[`hɛro,ɪn]
名 海洛英

Heroin is a very dangerous drug.
海洛因是一種非常危險的毒品。

envelop
[ɪn`vɛləp]
動 裹住

The mountaintop was enveloped in clouds.
山頂被雲霧籠罩。

derive
[dɪˋraɪv]
動 衍生

His name is derived from an African word.
他的名字衍生自一個非洲文字。

George
[dʒɔrdʒ]
名 喬治

George turned pro after he graduated from university.
喬治大學畢業後成為職業選手。

heaven
[ˋhɛvən]
名 天國

May his soul rest in Heaven.
願他的靈魂在天堂安息。

morale
[məˋræl]
名 士氣

Morale improved when the employees got raises.
員工加薪後士氣有所改善。

stripe
[straɪp]
名 條紋

Stripes look really good on you.
你穿條紋的衣服真好看。

freight
[fret]
名 貨運

When we move, let's send our furniture by freight.
搬家的時候，用貨運把家具送過去。

heroine
[ˋhɛro,ɪn]
名 女英雄

The heroine saved the people at the last minute.
女英雄在最後一刻救了大家。

envelope
[ˋɛnvə,lop]
名 信封

The envelope was addressed to my neighbor, but it was delivered to my house.
信封上的地址是我鄰居的，信卻寄到我家來。

想想看 要將填入的字改為合乎文法的形式喔！

下面這些句子少了哪個字？

moral	*wage*
scare	*unit*
ride	*fade*
past	*morale*

1. **The flowers on this tree blossom and then quickly _______.**
   這棵樹上的花開之後很快就會謝掉。

2. **The angry dog _______ many people.**
   那隻憤怒的狗令很多人害怕。

3. **He wasn't around for the _______ five years.**
   過去五年他人不在這裡。

4. **She sells the cups in _______ of six.**
   她以一組六個為單位出售杯子。

5. **Tina left her old job for a new one with a higher _______.**
   蒂娜為了一份比較高薪的工作離開舊職。

6. **He can _______ a horse.**
   他會騎馬。

7. **It's important that the soldiers have good _______.**
   軍隊士兵擁有良好士氣是很重要的。

找找看

以下句子在前面都出現過，你確定都讀熟了嗎？
找找看下面的句子有沒有拼錯的字。
錯字訂正於上方箭頭處，沒錯字請打“ ○ ”

下面哪些句子有字拼錯了？

8 →

He learned to shoot while in the corpse.

他入伍時學會射擊。

9 →

I can't see a thing in this dean light.

在這昏暗的燈光下，我什麼也看不到。

10 →

The dam was made to help control the river.

建這個水壩是為了控制這條河的流量。

11 →

Wearing a headband was a fade from the eighties.

戴頭巾是八〇年代的流行裝扮。

12 →

Beware of the gape when you get on the MRT.

上捷運列車時，要當心月台間隙。

13 →

Teenagers like to wear baseball capes.

青少年喜歡戴棒球帽。

1. fade
2. scares
3. past
4. units
5. wage
6. ride
7. morale
8. corpse → corps
9. dean → dim
10. ○
11. fade → fad
12. gape → gap
13. capes → caps

>>>翻譯解答

加碼字母 +F

試試看

把左邊的字加一個*f*，會變成什麼字？

lag	落後	⇨	***f*lag**
law	法律	⇨	***f*law**
owl	貓頭鷹	⇨	***f*owl**
lash	抽打	⇨	***f*lash**
rank	等級	⇨	***f*rank**
scar	疤	⇨	**scar*f***
actor	演員	⇨	***f*actor**
action	行動	⇨	***f*action**

MP3-213

lag
[læg]
動 落後

Our racing bike sales have been lagging behind our sales for recreational bikes.
我們的競賽用腳踏車銷售量一直落後休閒腳踏車的銷售量。

law
[lɔ]
名 法律

The traffic laws in this country are rarely enforced.
這個國家的交通法規執行成效不彰。

owl
[aʊl]
名 貓頭鷹

We saw an owl hiding in the barn.
我們看見一隻貓頭鷹躲在穀倉裡。

lash
[læʃ]
動 抽打

The man lashed the mule to make it walk faster.
男子鞭打騾子好讓牠走快一點。

rank
[ræŋk]
名 等級

You can tell the rank of a general by the number of stars on his uniform.
從軍服上的星星數量，可以分辨將軍的階級。

scar
[skɑr]
名 疤

The boy has a scar on his arm from where he cut himself.
男孩割傷自己時在手臂上留了一道疤。

actor
[`æktɚ]
名 演員

He won an Oscar for best actor in 2004.
他於二〇〇四年贏得奧斯卡最佳男主角獎。

action
[`ækʃən]
名 行動

There is very little action in this romance novel.
這本浪漫小說裡的動作場面很少。

flag
[flæg]
名 旗

We are holding our country's flag.
我們拿著我們的國旗。

flaw
[flɔ]
名 瑕疵

There's a large flaw in your reasoning.
你的推論有一個很大的瑕疵。

fowl
[faul]
名 家禽

Jews can eat beef and lamb, and any kind of fowl is OK.
猶太人可以吃牛肉和羊肉，所有鳥類的肉也都可以吃。

flash
[flæʃ]
名 閃光

We saw a flash of light in the sky.
我們看見空中有一道閃光。

frank
[fræŋk]
形 坦白的

To be frank, I am not interested in you as a girlfriend.
坦白說，我無意把妳當作女朋友。

scarf
[skɑrf]
名 圍巾

Mom knitted a scarf for me this winter.
媽媽今年冬天織了一條圍巾給我。

factor
[`fæktɚ]
名 因素

There are many factors that contribute to global warming.
許多原因造成全球暖化。

faction
[`fækʃən]
名 派別

This country's government is split into several factions.
這個國家的政府分裂成許多派系。

想想看 要將填入的字改為合乎文法的形式喔！

下面這些句子少了哪個字？

lag	*scarf*
flaw	*action*
factor	*fowl*
actor	*flash*

1. **It'd be good to wear a _______ today because it's windy and cold.**
今天最好披條圍巾出門，因為今天颳風又有點冷。

2. **The _______ that caused the experiment to fail is still unknown.**
造成實驗失敗的因素至今不明。

3. **All the stars _______ in the sky.**
滿天星斗在空中閃爍。

4. **The _______ was hired to play a role in the action movie.**
這個演員受雇飾演這部動作片的一個角色。

5. **There are several _______ on the surface of this table.**
這張桌子上有幾個瑕疵。

6. **His family raises _______ and pigs.**
他家飼養家禽和豬隻。

7. **There was a two-minute _______ in the runners' finishing times.**
跑者跑完的時間有兩分鐘的差距。

以下句子在前面都出現過，你確定都讀熟了嗎？
找找看下面的句子有沒有拼錯的字。
錯字訂正於上方箭頭處，沒錯字請打“○”

下面哪些句子有字拼錯了？

8 →

The boy has a scare on his arm from where he cut himself.

男孩割傷自己時在手臂上留了一道疤。

9 →

There's a large fowl in your reasoning.

你的推論有一個很大的瑕疵。

10 →

To be franking, I am not interested in you as a girlfriend.

坦白說，我無意把妳當作女朋友。

11 →

There are many factors that contribute to global warming.

許多原因造成全球暖化。

12 →

We saw a frank of light in the sky.

我們看見空中有一道閃光。

13 →

He won an Oscar for best acter in 2004.

他於二〇〇四年贏得奧斯卡最佳男主角獎。

1. scarf
2. factor
3. flash
4. actor
5. flaws
6. fowl
7. lag
8. scare → scar
9. fowl → flaw
10. franking → frank
11. ○
12. frank → flash
13. acter → actor

加碼字母 +G

試試看

把左邊的字加一個*g*，會變成什麼字？

fan	迷	→	**fan*g***
own	自己的	→	***g*own**
ram	公羊	→	***g*ram**
rim	邊緣	→	***g*rim**
loss	損失	→	***g*loss**
rain	雨	→	***g*rain**
lance	長矛	→	***g*lance**
litter	丟垃圾	→	***g*litter**

MP3-214

fan
[fæn]
名 迷

The popular singer has many fans.
這個受歡迎的歌手有好多歌迷。

own
[on]
形 自己的

I want to have my own house some day.
我希望有朝一日能擁有屬於自己的房子。

ram
[ræm]
名 公羊

The farmer has many sheep, but only one ram.
那個農夫有很多綿羊，但只有一隻公羊。

rim
[rɪm]
名 邊緣

They walked to the rim of the volcano and looked in.
他們走到火山口邊緣朝裡面看。

loss
[lɔs]
名 損失

They suffered great losses in the earthquake.
他們在地震中蒙受重大損失。

rain
[ren]
名 雨

The rain came and washed away all the soil.
這場雨沖刷掉所有土壤。

lance
[læns]
名 長矛

The men fought together with long lances.
那些男人持長矛互相鬥毆。

litter
[`lɪtɚ]
動 丟垃圾

Don’t litter in the park.
別在公園裡亂丟垃圾。

fang
[fæŋ]
名 毒牙

The spider has long fangs it uses to kill its prey.
蜘蛛用毒牙來殺死獵物。

gown
[gaʊn]
名（女用）長禮服

Bernice arrived at the party wearing a beautiful evening gown.
柏妮絲穿著一件很美的晚禮服抵達舞會。

gram
[græm]
名 公克

One thousand grams is equal to one kilogram.
一千公克相當於一公斤。

grim
[grɪm]
形 殘忍無情的

She had a grim expression when she told us of the accident.
她告訴我們那個意外時，表情很冷酷。

gloss
[glɔs]
名 亮光漆

He put a new gloss onto the old table.
他在舊桌子上塗上一層新的亮光漆。

grain
[gren]
名 穀類

Lots of grains are stored in the barn.
穀倉裡儲存了很多穀物。

glance
[glæns]
名 一瞥

I gave a quick glance at the passer-by.
我匆匆看了那個路人一眼。

glitter
[ˋglɪtɚ]
名 閃光

Did you put glitter in your lip gloss?
妳在唇彩裡加了亮粉？

想想看 要將填入的字改為合乎文法的形式喔！

下面這些句子少了哪個字？

grain	*glitter*
litter	*lance*
gram	*gown*
fan	*fang*

1. **She bought 200 _______ of cheddar cheese.**
   她買了兩百公克的卻達起司。

2. **He is a baseball _______.**
   他是一個棒球迷。

3. **Wheat is a very common _______.**
   小麥是一種很常見的穀類。

4. **The policeman caught my friend _______.**
   警察抓到我的朋友亂丟垃圾。

5. **The woman chose to wear a _______ to the dinner party.**
   那名女子選擇穿長禮服參加晚宴。

6. **The kids decorated their cards with _______.**
   孩子們用亮片裝飾他們做的卡片。

7. **The knights fought each other with _______.**
   中古騎士用長矛互相鬥毆。

找找看

以下句子在前面都出現過，你確定都讀熟了嗎？
找找看下面的句子有沒有拼錯的字。
錯字訂正於上方箭頭處，沒錯字請打“○”

下面哪些句子有字拼錯了？

8 →

They walked to the ram of the volcano and looked in.

他們走到火山口邊緣朝裡面看。

9 →

The popular singer has many fans.

這個受歡迎的歌手有好多歌迷。

10 →

The spider has long fans it uses to kill its prey.

蜘蛛用毒牙來殺死獵物。

11 →

One thousand gram is equal to one kilogram.

一千公克相當於一公斤。

12 →

I gave a quick gloss at the passerby.

我匆匆看了那個路人一眼。

13 →

Don't litter in the park.

別在公園亂丟垃圾。

1. grams
2. fan
3. grain
4. littering
5. gown
6. glitter
7. lances

8. ram → rim
9. ○
10. fans → fangs
11. gram → grams
12. gloss → glance
13. ○

加碼字母

+H

試試看

把左邊的字加一個*h*，會變成什麼字？

ace	么點牌	**ac*h*e**	
are	是	***h*are**	
art	藝術	***h*art**	
oat	燕麥	**oat*h***	
pat	輕拍	**pat*h***	
aunt	阿姨	***h*aunt**	
Coke	可口可樂	**c*h*oke**	
cord	細繩	**c*h*ord**	

試試看

把右邊的字減一個*h*，會變成什麼字？

edge	→	***h*edge** 籬笆
itch	→	***h*itch** 搭便車
over	→	***h*over** 盤旋
tank	→	**t*h*ank** 感謝
tick	→	**t*h*ick** 厚的
heart	→	**heart*h*** 爐邊
tread	→	**t*h*read** 線
trust	→	**t*h*rust** 刺

MP3-215

ace
[es]
名 么點牌

The magician found all four aces.
魔術師找出了撲克牌中全部四張A。

are
[ɑr]
動 是

We are waiting for a letter from headquarters to arrive.
我們正在等總部寄來的信。

art
[ɑrt]
名 藝術

The boy enjoys the art classes he attends after school.
男孩很喜歡他放學後上的美術課。

oat
[ot]
名 燕麥

The farmer bought a lot of oats.
農夫買了很多燕麥。

pat
[pæt]
動 輕拍

She patted the dough down before baking it.
她把麵糰拍扁之後再烤。

aunt
[ænt]
名 阿姨

His aunt is a famous author who has written many books.
她的阿姨是位知名作家，已經寫了好幾本書。

Coke
[kok]
名 可口可樂

Coke is not very healthy, but it's still the world's most popular drink.
可口可樂對健康不太好，但依然是全球最受歡迎的飲料。

cord
[kɔrd]
名 細繩

She tied the gift closed with a cord.
她用細繩把禮物綁緊。

ache
[ek]
動 疼痛

My back has been aching all day.
我的背已經痛了一整天。

hare
[hɛr]
名 野兔

The hare saw the hunter and ran.
野兔看見獵人就跑掉了。

hart
[hɑrt]
名 雄鹿

They spotted a hart in the forest.
他們在森林裡看見一隻雄鹿。

oath
[oθ]
名 誓言

He took an oath before becoming a doctor.
他在成為醫生之前宣誓過。

path
[pæθ]
名 小路

There is a little path leading to the riverside.
有一條小徑通往河邊。

haunt
[hɔnt]
名 常去的地方

This bar is our favorite haunt.
這家酒吧是我們最愛去光顧的地方。

choke
[tʃok]
動 窒息

The victim was choked by the heavy smoke.
罹難者是被濃煙嗆死的。

chord
[kɔrd]
名 和弦

He showed me how to play a chord on the guitar.
他教我怎麼彈奏吉他和弦。

MP3-216

edge
[ɛdʒ]
名 邊緣

The diver jumped off the cliff edge and into the ocean.
跳水者從懸崖邊跳入海中。

itch
[ɪtʃ]
名 癢

I had to take off my shoe to scratch an itch on my foot.
我得把鞋脫掉才能抓到腳癢的地方。

over
[`ovɚ]
介 超過

Over thirty people applied for the job.
超過三十個人應徵那份工作。

tank
[tæŋk]
名 油箱

The tank was nearly empty when we found a gas station.
我們找到加油站時油箱幾乎見底了。

tick
[tɪk]
動 發滴答聲

He heard a ticking sound coming from the suitcase.
他聽到公事包裡傳出滴答聲。

heart
[hɑrt]
名 心，心臟

The doctor said that the old man's heart is still in good condition.
醫生說這個老人的心臟狀況還很好。

tread
[trɛd]
動 踩

Please be careful not to tread on these flowers.
請小心不要踩到這些花。

trust
[trʌst]
動 信任

Daddy wouldn't trust me with his car.
爸爸不放心把車交給我。

hedge
[hɛdʒ]
名 籬笆

The shrubs will look marvelous around the hedges.
這些灌木種在樹籬邊會很好看。

hitch
[hɪtʃ]
動 搭便車

He hitched a ride to Houston.
他搭便車前往休士頓。

hover
[ˋhʌvɚ]
動 盤旋

The bird seemed to hover in the air.
那隻鳥似乎在空中盤旋。

thank
[θæŋk]
動 感謝

I'd like to thank you for all of the assistance you've given me.
我要感謝你給予我的所有協助。

thick
[θɪk]
形 厚的

How thick is this cutting board?
這個砧板有多厚？

hearth
[hɑrθ]
名 爐邊

They dried their clothes on the hearth.
他們在爐邊烘乾衣物。

thread
[θrɛd]
名 線

The jobless young man didn't have a thread of hope.
這個失業青年沒有一線希望。

thrust
[θrʌst]
動 刺

He thrust the knife forward but missed his target.
他向前刺一刀，但沒刺中目標。

想想看 要將填入的字改為合乎文法的形式喔！

下面這些句子少了哪個字？

thrust	*thick*
path	*choke*
thread	*over*
chord	*tank*

1. **The man almost _______ while eating pretzels.**
   那個男的吃椒鹽脆餅時差點嗆死。

2. **My friend taught me how to play a _______ on the guitar.**
   我朋友教我用吉他彈一個和弦。

3. **The dark clouds floated _______ the mountain.**
   山頂上烏雲密布。

4. **She tied a _______ to her finger to remind her to do something.**
   她在手指上綁一條線來提醒自己做某件事。

5. **This _______ will lead you to the lake.**
   這條小徑會通往湖邊。

6. **That shirt is made of _______ cloth.**
   那件襯衫是用厚布料作成的。

7. **She has shrimp and starfish in that _______.**
   她在水槽裡養蝦和海星。

找找看

以下句子在前面都出現過，你確定都讀熟了嗎？
找找看下面的句子有沒有拼錯的字。
錯字訂正於上方箭頭處，沒錯字請打"○"

下面哪些句子有字拼錯了？

8 →

The victim was coked by the heavy smoke.

罹難者是被濃煙嗆死的。

9 →

The boy enjoys the art classes he attends after school.

男孩很喜歡他放學後上的美術課。

10 →

She tied the gift closed with a chord.

她用細繩把禮物綁緊。

11 →

He trust the knife forward but missed his target.

他向前刺一刀但沒刺中目標。

12 →

This bar is our favorite hunt.

這家酒吧是我們最愛去光顧的地方。

13 →

He heard a thicking sound coming from the suitcase.

他聽到公事包裡傳出滴答聲。

1. choked
2. chord
3. over
4. thread
5. path
6. thick
7. tank
8. coked → choked
9. ○
10. chord → cord
11. trust → thrust
12. hunt → haunt
13. thicking → ticking

>>>測驗解答

加碼字母 +I

試試看

把左邊的字加一個*i*，會變成什麼字？

van	廂形車	→	**va*i*n**
bran	穀皮	→	**bra*i*n**
char	燒焦	→	**cha*i*r**
maze	迷宮	→	**ma*i*ze**
span	跨越	→	**Spa*i*n**
wave	波浪	→	**wa*i*ve**
savor	風味	→	**sav*i*or**
patent	專利	→	**pat*i*ent**

MP3-217

van
[væn]
名 廂形車

The school uses vans to transfer students.
學校用廂型車載運學生。

bran
[bræn]
名 穀皮

This muffin is made from bran.
這塊杯子蛋糕是用麥麩做成的。

char
[tʃɑr]
動 燒焦

The steak he made was quite charred.
他煎的牛排很焦。

maze
[mez]
名 迷宮

The child drew mazes in his notebook.
那個孩子在他的筆記本裡畫了一座迷宮。

span
[spæn]
動 跨越

This road spans the entire country.
這條路跨越整個國土。

wave
[wev]
動 揮（手）

We waved from the ship as it left the dock.
船要離岸時，我們在船上揮手。

savor
[`sevɚ]
名 風味

She enjoys the special savor of Thai food.
她很喜歡泰國料理的特殊風味。

patent
[`pætn̩t]
名 專利

He applied for a patent for his new invention.
他為他的新發明申請專利。

vain
[ven]
形 徒然的

His efforts to change my opinion were all in vain.
他試圖改變我的想法卻完全徒勞無功。

brain
[bren]
名 頭腦

Let's just say he's running low in the brains department.
我們姑且說他腦袋少根筋吧。

chair
[tʃɛr]
名 椅子

We don't have enough chairs for ten people.
我們的椅子不夠十個人坐。

maize
[mez]
名 玉蜀黍

Maize is a kind of wild corn.
maize是一種野生玉米。

Spain
[spen]
名 西班牙

Bull fights are still popular in Spain.
鬥牛在西班牙仍然很流行。

waive
[wev]
動 放棄

Some of the requirements for this class have been waived.
這堂課的一些門檻都取消了。

savior
[`sevjɚ]
名 救助者

Her savior came and rescued her from the burning building.
救她的人把她從失火的大樓中救出來。

patient
[`peʃənt]
名 病人

What happened to that crazy patient?
那個瘋狂的病人怎麼了？

想想看 要將填入的字改為合乎文法的形式喔！

下面這些句子少了哪個字？

patent	*brain*
vain	*waive*
savior	*patient*
savor	*maze*

❶ **The man was praised as a ______ after he put out the fire.**
那個男子把火撲滅之後，被誇獎是救命恩人。

❷ **Humans have large ______ compared to our body size.**
相較於身體尺寸，人類的腦很大。

❸ **When the fire broke out, ______ in the hospital all ran out.**
火災發生時，醫院裡所有病患都跑出來了。

❹ **The chef ______ the taste of his newest dish.**
主廚細細品味他最新推出的菜餚。

❺ **This company has a ______ on a new kind of battery.**
這家公司擁有一種新型電池的專利。

❻ **The ______ man can only talk about himself.**
那個自負的男人講話只會繞著自己打轉。

❼ **The workers ______ their right to a salary increase.**
勞工為了加薪放棄自己的權益。

找找看

以下句子在前面都出現過，你確定都讀熟了嗎？
找找看下面的句子有沒有拼錯的字。
錯字訂正於上方箭頭處，沒錯字請打"○"

下面哪些句子有字拼錯了？

8 →

He applied for a patient for his new invention.

他為他的新發明申請專利。

9 →

What happened to that crazy patent?

那個瘋狂的病人怎麼了？

10 →

We wave from the ship as it left the dock.

船要離岸時，我們在船上揮手。

11 →

She enjoys the special savior of Thai food.

她很喜歡泰國料理的特殊風味。

12 →

This muffin is made from brain.

這塊杯子蛋糕是用麥麩做成的。

13 →

His efforts to change my opinion were all in van.

他試圖改變我的想法卻完全徒勞無功。

1. savior
2. brains
3. patients
4. savored
5. patent
6. vain
7. waived
8. patient → patent
9. patent → patient
10. wave → waved
11. savior → savor
12. brain → bran
13. van → vain

加碼字母 +L

試試看

把左邊的字加一個*l*，會變成什麼字？

bow	弓	→	**bow*l***	
due	因為	→	**due*l***	
ear	耳朵	→	**ear*l***	
how	怎樣	→	**how*l***	
woo	求愛	→	**woo*l***	
bond	債券	→	**b*l*ond**	
ease	容易	→	**ease*l***	
fare	票價	→	**f*l*are**	

試試看

把右邊的字減一個*l*，會變成什麼字？

grow	grow*l* 嗥叫
mode	mode*l* 模特兒
pane	pane*l* 嵌板
push	p*l*ush 豪華的
caste	cast*l*e 城堡
grave	grave*l* 碎石
peasant	p*l*easant 令人愉快的
strange	strang*l*e 勒死

MP3-218

bow
[baʊ]
名 弓

The hunter made a bow from a tree branch.
這個獵人用樹枝做成一把弓。

due
[dju]
形 因為

Due to the heavy rain, lots of students were late to school.
因為這場大雨，很多學生上學遲到。

ear
[ɪr]
名 耳朵

This breed of dog has long, floppy ears.
這個品種的狗耳朵又長又軟。

how
[haʊ]
副 怎樣

Do you know how to get there?
你知道如何去那裡嗎？

woo
[wu]
動 求愛

Her suitor wooed her from morning until night.
她的愛慕者從早到晚都在向她求婚。

bond
[bɑnd]
名 公債

All of my extra earnings are invested in stocks and bonds.
我多賺的錢都投入股票和債券了。

ease
[iz]
名 容易

She sang the song with ease.
她從容地唱那首歌。

fare
[fɛr]
名 票價

The ticket fare to New York is not cheap.
到紐約的票價並不便宜。

bowl
[bol]
名 碗

She placed her spare change in a bowl on the shelf.
她把多餘的零錢放在架子上的碗裡。

duel
[`djuəl]
名 決鬥

The men had a duel with swords.
那些男人用劍決鬥。

earl
[ɝl]
名 伯爵

He met an earl when he lived in England.
他住在英國時遇見一位公爵。

howl
[haul]
動 吠叫，嚎叫

The dog howls whenever its owner leaves it.
那隻狗只要主人一離開就會吠叫。

wool
[wul]
名 羊毛

Wool is used to make lots of things, like socks and hats.
羊毛被用來作成很多東西，像是襪子和帽子。

blond
[blɑnd]
形 金黃色的

You look younger with those blond highlights in your hair.
頭髮挑染成金色讓你看來更年輕。

easel
[`izl]
名 畫架

The artist brought his easel to the river to paint.
那位畫家帶著畫架到河邊作畫。

flare
[flɛr]
名 照明彈

They used a flare to attract attention.
他們用照明彈吸引注意力。

MP3-219

grow
[gro]
動 生長

Sean grows so fast; he is even taller than his father.
尚恩長得好快；他甚至比他的父親還高了。

mode
[mod]
名 方法

Walking is the slowest mode of travel.
步行是最慢的旅行方式。

pane
[pen]
名 窗玻璃片

He bought another pane of glass to replace the window.
他買了另一片玻璃裝回窗戶上。

push
[pʊʃ]
動 推開

Don't push in the hallway.
不要在走廊上推擠。

caste
[kæst]
名 等級制度

India is known for its caste system.
印度因階級制度而聞名。

grave
[grev]
名 墓穴

The thieves dug into the grave and stole the gold.
盜賊挖洞進墳墓，偷走了金子。

peasant
[`pɛzənt]
名 農夫

Peasants are people with very little money.
佃農是很窮的人。

strange
[strendʒ]
形 奇怪的

It's so strange that I failed my exam.
我考試竟然會不及格，真是奇怪。

growl
[graul]
動 嗥叫

The dog growled and scared me.
狗嗥叫時嚇到我了。

model
[`mad!]
名 模特兒

The young fashion model doesn't even know how to walk on the runway.
年輕模特兒連如何在伸展台上走台步都不會。

panel
[`pæn!]
名 嵌板

This car has a very nice instrument panel.
這輛車配備很棒的儀表板。

plush
[plʌʃ]
形 豪華的

She lives in a plush apartment on the top floor.
她住在一間位於頂樓的豪華公寓。

castle
[`kæs!]
名 城堡

Children like to build sand castles at the beach.
小孩喜歡在沙灘上蓋沙堡。

gravel
[`grævl]
名 碎石

The road is covered in gravel.
路上鋪了一層碎石子。

pleasant
[`plɛznt]
形 令人愉快的

We had a pleasant evening at the party.
我們在宴會上度過愉快的夜晚。

strangle
[`stræŋg!]
動 勒死

Police think the man was strangled.
警方認為那個男子是被勒死的。

想想看 要將填入的字改為合乎文法的形式喔！

下面這些句子少了哪個字？

grave	*growl*
fare	*model*
blond	*strangle*
castle	*bow*

1. **She wanted to be a _______ but she is too tall.**
   她想要成為模特兒，但是她太高了。

2. **The large snake _______ animals before swallowing them.**
   大蛇吞食動物前，會先將牠們勒死。

3. **The king and queen live in a _______.**
   國王和王后住在城堡裡。

4. **The bus _______ in the city will soon be more expensive.**
   城裡的公車票價很快就要調漲。

5. **There is a large _______ behind Mike's house.**
   麥克的房子後面有一座很大的墳墓。

6. **The young man asked her to dance with a polite _______.**
   年輕男子禮貌地鞠躬邀她跳舞。

7. **All three of his sisters have _______ hair.**
   他的三個姊妹都是金髮。

找找看

以下句子在前面都出現過，你確定都讀熟了嗎？
找找看下面的句子有沒有拼錯的字。
錯字訂正於上方箭頭處，沒錯字請打"○"

下面哪些句子有字拼錯了？

8 →

This car has a very nice instrument pane.

這輛車配備很棒的儀表板。

9 →

She placed her spare change in a bow on the shelf.

她把多餘的零錢放在架子上的碗裡。

10 →

All of my extra earnings are invested in stocks and bonds.

我多賺的錢都投入股票和債券了。

11 →

The ticket fair to New York is not cheap.

到紐約的票價並不便宜。

12 →

Police think the man was stranged.

警方認為那個男子是被勒死的。

13 →

The dog growled and scared me.

狗嗥叫時嚇到我了。

❶ model
❷ strangles
❸ castle
❹ fare
❺ grave
❻ bow
❼ blond
❽ pane → panel
❾ bow → bowl
❿ ○
⓫ fair → fare
⓬ stranged → strangled
⓭ ○

>>>測驗解答

加碼字母

+M

試試看

把左邊的字加一個*m*，會變成什麼字？

are	是	➡	***m*are**
end	結束	➡	***m*end**
ink	墨水	➡	***m*ink**
nor	也不	➡	**nor*m***
coma	昏迷	➡	**com*m*a**
oral	口頭的	➡	***m*oral**
real	真的	➡	**real*m***
anger	生氣	➡	***m*anger**

MP3-220

are
[ɑr]
動 是

We are in the train station awaiting the arrival of our family.
我們在火車站等待家人到來。

end
[ɛnd]
名 結束

The end of the story is surprising and sad.
這個故事的結局令人驚訝又悲傷。

ink
[ɪŋk]
名 墨水

She purchased more ink with which to finish her painting.
她為了完成畫作買了更多墨水。

nor
[nɔr]
連 也不

Mary didn't do homework, nor did Tony.
瑪莉沒做功課，東尼也沒做。

coma
[`komə]
名 昏迷

My cousin went into a coma after the accident.
那次意外之後，我表姊就陷入昏迷。

oral
[`orəl]
形 口頭的

The oral part of this exam requires us to converse with our teacher in English.
這個測驗的口說部分要我們跟老師用英文對話。

real
[riəl]
形 真的

I thought the flowers were real, but they are in fact fake.
我以為這些花是真的，但其實是假的。

anger
[`æŋgɚ]
名 生氣

His anger was evidenced by the redness of his face.
他滿面通紅就是他生氣的證明。

mare
[mɛr]
名 母馬

The mare slept in the field in the sun.
母馬在陽光照耀的原野上睡覺。

mend
[mɛnd]
動 修理

The farmer spent several days mending fences after the storm.
暴風雨過後，農夫花了好幾天修復籬笆。

mink
[mɪŋk]
名 貂

They found a mink running near the pond.
他們發現一隻貂在池塘附近奔跑。

norm
[nɔrm]
名 規範，基準

You must conform to our group's norms.
你必須符合我們這個團體的規範。

comma
[`kɑmə]
名 逗號

The sentence needs another comma in the middle.
這個句子中間需要再加一個逗號。

moral
[`mɔrəl]
名 道德

It's nice to read stories with morals to children.
讀具有道德教訓的故事給孩子聽很不錯。

realm
[rɛlm]
名 領域，王國

His stories take place in fictional realms.
他的故事發生在虛構的環境裡。

manger
[`mendʒɚ]
名 馬槽

The horses have been tied in the manger.
有幾匹馬被綁在馬槽邊。

想想看 要將填入的字改為合乎文法的形式喔！

下面這些句子少了哪個字？

realm	*mink*
moral	*end*
nor	*comma*
anger	*oral*

1. **I want this difficult day to _______!**
   我希望過完這難熬的一天！

2. **She is neither rich _______ famous.**
   她既不有錢也不有名。

3. **The story takes place in a _______ of fantasy and magic.**
   這個故事發生在一個奇幻與魔法王國。

4. **The Chinese and English languages use _______ very differently.**
   中文和英文使用逗號的方法非常不同。

5. **The farmer raises _______ to be sold for fur.**
   農夫養貂來賣皮毛。

6. **His _______ grew the more he thought about his situation.**
   他越去想他遭遇的情況就越生氣。

7. **"Do not lie" is a common _______ in many stories.**
   「不要說謊」是許多故事裡常見的道德教訓。

找找看

以下句子在前面都出現過，你確定都讀熟了嗎？
找找看下面的句子有沒有拼錯的字。
錯字訂正於上方箭頭處，沒錯字請打"○"

下面哪些句子有字拼錯了？

8 →

His stories take place in fictional reams.

他的故事發生在虛構的環境裡。

9 →

It's nice to read stories with morals to children.

讀具有道德教訓的故事給孩子聽很不錯。

10 →

I thought the flowers were really, but they are in fact fake.

我以為這些花是真的，但其實是假的

11 →

His anger was evidenced by the redness of his face.

他滿面通紅就是他生氣的證據。

12 →

Mary didn't do homework, no did Tony.

瑪莉沒做功課，東尼也沒做。

13 →

The sentence needs another coma in the middle.

這個句子中間需要再加一個逗號。

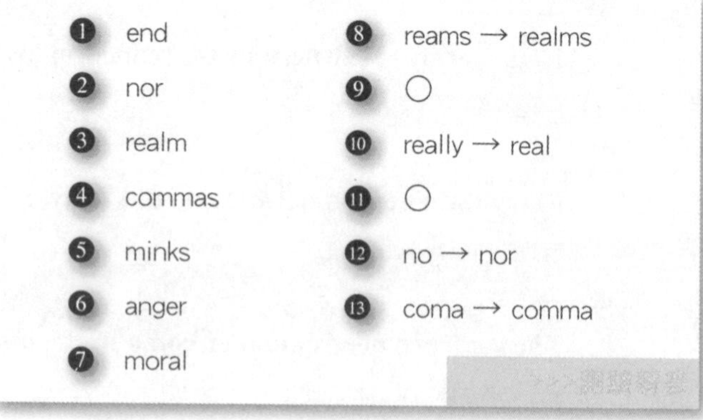

1. end
2. nor
3. realm
4. commas
5. minks
6. anger
7. moral
8. reams → realms
9. ○
10. really → real
11. ○
12. no → nor
13. coma → comma

加碼字母 +N

試試看

把左邊的字加一個*n*，會變成什麼字？

ace	么點牌	→	**ac*n*e**
paw	爪子	→	**paw*n***
doze	打瞌睡	→	**doze*n***
line	隊伍	→	**line*n***
sore	疼痛	→	**s*n*ore**
year	年	→	**year*n***
ethic	倫理標準	→	**eth*n*ic**
metal	金屬	→	**me*n*tal**

MP3-221

ace
[es]
名 么點牌

He found the ace of hearts under the table.
他在桌子底下發現紅心A。

paw
[pɔ]
名 爪子

The cat got injured paws.
貓的爪子受傷了。

doze
[doz]
動 打瞌睡

I dozed off when I was on the bus.
我搭公車時打起瞌睡來。

line
[laɪn]
名 隊伍

Hundreds of people were waiting in line at the Disneyland rides.
數百人在排隊等著搭迪士尼樂園的遊樂設施。

sore
[sor]
名 疼痛

He has a sore on his foot from walking so much.
他因為走太多路而腳痛。

year
[jɪr]
名 年

I've stayed in Taiwan for three years.
我已經在台灣住三年了。

ethic
[`ɛθɪk]
名 倫理標準

Children usually learn ethics from their friends and families.
孩子通常從朋友和家人那兒學到倫理觀念。

metal
[`mɛtl̩]
名 金屬

Would you like your picture frame to be made of wood or metal?
你的相框要用木頭還是金屬材質？

acne
[ˋæknɪ]
名 粉刺

The doctor looked at his zits and gave him some new acne medication.
醫生幫他檢查青春痘，並且開給他一些新的治粉刺藥物。

pawn
[pɔn]
動 典當

He pawned his watch and got fifty dollars.
他把手錶當掉，得到五十元美金。

dozen
[ˋdʌzn̩]
名 一打

Grandma needs a dozen eggs to bake a cake.
奶奶需要一打雞蛋來烤蛋糕。

linen
[ˋlɪnən]
名 亞麻布

Clothes made of linen wrinkle easily.
亞麻布製的衣服很容易皺。

snore
[snor]
動 打鼾

He was snoring loudly all night long.
他整晚都大聲打鼾。

yearn
[jɝn]
動 思念，嚮往

She yearns for the company of her old friends.
她很想念這家公司的老朋友。

ethnic
[ˋɛθnɪk]
形 種族(上)的

What is your ethnic make-up?
你具有哪些血統？

mental
[ˋmɛntl̩]
形 精神的

The girl went to see a doctor for her mental illness.
這女孩因為心理疾病去看醫生。

想想看 要將填入的字改為合乎文法的形式喔！

下面這些句子少了哪個字？

acne	*dozen*
ace	*snore*
linen	*line*
mental	*metal*

❶ **The _______ for the roller-coaster is very long.**
排隊要玩雲霄飛車的隊伍很長。

❷ **This doctor specializes in treating _______ patients.**
這位醫師的專長是治療精神病患。

❸ **The teenager no longer has a problem with _______.**
那個少年不再有長粉刺的困擾。

❹ **It was hard to sleep with that guy _______ so loudly.**
跟那個鼾聲大作的人共寢很難睡著。

❺ **He won the hand with three aces.**
他拿三張**A**贏了那一手牌。

❻ **The _______ chair is strong enough for the fat man.**
這張金屬材質的椅子對那個胖子來說夠堅固。

❼ **She bought a _______ eggs to make several cakes.**
她買了一打雞蛋來做幾個蛋糕。

找找看

以下句子在前面都出現過，你確定都讀熟了嗎？
找找看下面的句子有沒有拼錯的字。
錯字訂正於上方箭頭處，沒錯字請打“ ○ ”

下面哪些句子有字拼錯了？

8 →

He found the ase of hearts under the table.

他在桌子底下發現紅心A。

9 →

Grandma needs a dozen eggs to bake a cake.

奶奶需要一打雞蛋來烤蛋糕。

10 →

He was soring loudly all night long.

他整晚都大聲打鼾。

11 →

I doze off when I was on the bus.

我搭公車時打了瞌睡。

12 →

What is your ethic make-up?

你具有哪些血統？

13 →

Would you like your picture frame to be made of wood or mental?

你的相框要用木頭還是金屬材質？

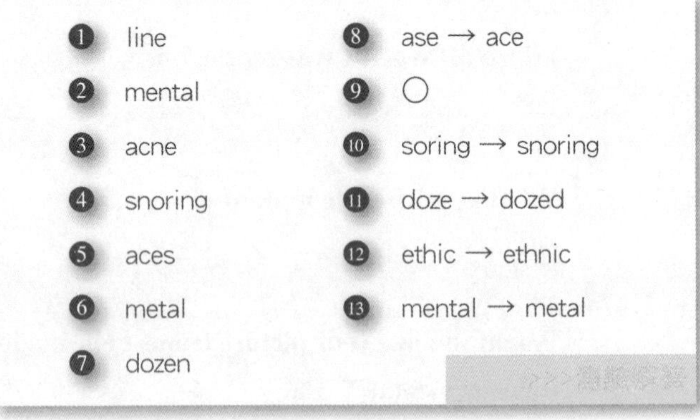

1. line
2. mental
3. acne
4. snoring
5. aces
6. metal
7. dozen
8. ase → ace
9. ○
10. soring → snoring
11. doze → dozed
12. ethic → ethnic
13. mental → metal

加碼字母 +O

試試看

把左邊的字加一個*o*，會變成什麼字？

man	男人	→	**m*o*an**
ram	公羊	→	**r*o*am**
both	兩者	→	**b*o*oth**
envy	妒忌	→	**env*o*y**
zone	地區	→	***o*zone**
muse	冥想	→	**m*o*use**
being	人	→	**B*o*eing**
carton	紙板箱	→	**cart*o*on**

MP3-222

man
[mæn]
名 男人

That man over there is looking for a taxi.
那邊那個男人正在叫計程車。

ram
[ræm]
名 公羊

The farmer bought a ram to keep on his farm.
農夫買了一隻公羊養在農場裡。

both
[boθ]
代 兩者

Both of them are late.
他們倆都遲到了。

envy
[`ɛnvɪ]
動 妒忌

All the students envy his opportunity to dine with a movie star.
學生們無不羨慕他有機會與一個電影明星共進晚餐。

zone
[zon]
名 地區

The countries are working to establish a free trade zone.
這幾個國家正在預備建造一個自由貿易區。

muse
[mjuz]
名 冥想

He mused at the amount of money spent on the plan.
他暗自盤算這個計畫已花掉多少錢。

being
[`biɪŋ]
名 人

Human beings first lived in Africa.
人類一開始居住在非洲。

carton
[`kɑrtn̩]
名 紙板箱，紙盒

How much does a carton of eggs cost?
一盒雞蛋多少錢？

moan
[mon]
動 呻吟

I've been hearing this groaning and moaning every other night.
我每隔一天晚上就會聽到這種呻吟哀號的聲音。

roam
[rom]
動 漫遊

I want to roam across the world.
我想到世界各地漫遊。

booth
[buθ]
名 雅座

These booths are so comfortable.
這些包廂好舒服。

envoy
[`ɛnvɔɪ]
名 外交使節

A United Nations envoy was sent to talk to the country's leaders.
一名聯合國大使被派去跟這位國家領導人對談。

ozone
[`ozon]
名 臭氧

Styrofoam releases chemicals that damage the ozone layer.
保麗龍釋放的化學物質會破壞臭氧層。

mouse
[maʊs]
名 老鼠

Most children love Mickey Mouse.
大多數小孩都喜歡米老鼠。

Boeing
[`boɪŋ]
名 波音公司

Boeing is one of the world's largest airplane manufacturers.
波音公司是世界上最大的飛機製造商之一。

cartoon
[kɑr`tun]
名 卡通

The children watch cartoons on Saturday morning.
小孩子在星期六早上看卡通。

想想看 要將填入的字改為合乎文法的形式喔！

下面這些句子少了哪個字？

carton	*mouse*
booth	*both*
zone	*moan*
ozone	*cartoon*

1. **They all _______ when they heard they'd have to work overtime.**
他們聽到要加班時都發出哀嚎。

2. **_______ of his brothers are also lawyers.**
他的兩個兄弟也都是律師。

3. **They were sitting in a _______ by the window when they saw the accident.**
他們目睹意外發生時，正坐在餐廳靠窗的雅座裡。

4. **She purchased a _______ of candy bars before Halloween.**
她在萬聖節前買了一大箱巧克力棒。

5. **_______ are watched mainly by children.**
卡通主要是小孩子在看的。

6. **No businesses are allowed in the city's residential _______.**
城裡的住宅區不可以開設公司行號。

7. **_______ is made up of three parts oxygen.**
臭氧是由三個氧分子構成。

找找看

以下句子在前面都出現過，你確定都讀熟了嗎？
找找看下面的句子有沒有拼錯的字。
錯字訂正於上方箭頭處，沒錯字請打“ ○ ”

下面哪些句子有字拼錯了？

8 →

Styrofoam releases chemicals that damage the ozon layer.

保麗龍釋放的化學物質會破壞臭氧層。

9 →

How much does a cartoon of eggs cost?

一盒雞蛋多少錢？

10 →

I've been hearing this groaning and roaming every other night.

我每隔一天晚上就會聽到一種呻吟哀號的聲音。

11 →

The countries are working to establish a free trade zone.

這幾個國家正在預備建造一個自由貿易區。

12 →

These boths are so comfortable.

這些包廂好舒服。

13 →

All the students envy his opportunity to dine with a movie star.

學生們無不羨慕他有機會與一個電影明星共進晚餐。

1. moaned
2. Both
3. booth
4. carton
5. Cartoons
6. zones
7. Ozone
8. ozon → ozone
9. cartoon → carton
10. roaming → moaning
11. ○
12. boths → booths
13. envoy → envy

加碼字母 +P

試試看

把左邊的字加一個*p*，會變成什麼字？

at	在…（地點）	→	**a*p*t**
clam	蛤蜊	→	**clam*p***
cram	死記硬背	→	**cram*p***
itch	癢	→	***p*itch**
reach	達到	→	***p*reach**
resent	怨恨	→	***p*resent**
article	文章	→	***p*article**
resident	居民	→	***p*resident**

MP3-223

at

[æt]

介 在…（地點）

Please arrive at 5 o'clock sharp.

請於五點整準時到達。

clam

[klæm]

名 蛤蜊

She baked clams and served them for dinner.

她烤蛤蜊當晚餐。

cram

[kræm]

名 死記硬背

I figured out the best method to cram all this information in my head in the shortest time possible.

我想出用最短時間讀完這一大堆資料的最佳方法。

itch

[ɪtʃ]

動 癢

Don't touch that plant. If you do, it will make you itch.

別碰那株植物。碰了的話，它會讓你發癢。

reach

[ritʃ]

動 達到

We have reached the top of the mountain.

我們已經抵達山頂。

resent

[rɪˋzɛnt]

動 怨恨

She resents her sister for her success.

她因為她姊姊的成功而怨恨她。

article

[ˋɑrtɪkḷ]

名 文章

Your articles have given me so many ideas!

妳的文章給了我好多點子！

resident

[ˋrɛzədənt]

名 居民

The bad news sparked anger in the residents of the city.

那個壞消息激起了這個城市居民憤怒的情緒。

apt
[æpt]
形 易於…的

They finally found a more apt description of the situation.
他們終於找到更容易描述整個情況的說法。

clamp
[klæmp]
動 夾住

The part is clamped to the machine.
那個零件被夾在機器上。

cramp
[kræmp]
動 抽筋

My leg muscle is cramping.
我的腿部肌肉抽筋了。

pitch
[pɪtʃ]
動 投擲

He pitched the ball and the batter hit it.
他投球出去，打擊者打到了球。

preach
[pritʃ]
動 說教

Father Paul preaches at his church on Sundays.
保羅神父星期天在他的教堂講道。

present
[ˋprɛzn̩t]
動 介紹

She presented her friend to the group.
她把她的朋友介紹給這個團體。

particle
[ˋpɑrtɪk!]
名 微粒

There are some particles in this bottle of wine.
這瓶葡萄酒有些微粒。

president
[ˋprɛzədənt]
名 總統

She's the first female president.
她是第一位女總統。

想想看 要將填入的字改為合乎文法的形式喔！

下面這些句子少了哪個字？

resident	*president*
itch	*article*
present	*cramp*
pitch	*reach*

1. **The lawyer _______ the judge with lots of evidence.**
   律師向法官出示多項證據。

2. **She had a _______ after swimming for just a few minutes.**
   她才游泳幾分鐘就抽筋了。

3. **I have an _______ on my back.**
   我背上有個地方好癢。

4. **They _______ their sales goals for the last three months.**
   他們最後三個月的業績目標達成了。

5. **The _______ have been warned about the approaching storm.**
   地方居民被警告有暴風雨即將來臨。

6. **She wrote an _______ for the school's newspaper.**
   她幫校刊寫了一篇文章。

7. **The _______ of the company just held a meeting with shareholders.**
   這家公司的總經理剛召開一場股東會議。

找找看 +

以下句子在前面都出現過，你確定都讀熟了嗎？
找找看下面的句子有沒有拼錯的字。
錯字訂正於上方箭頭處，沒錯字請打“○”

下面哪些句子有字拼錯了？

8 →

Your articles have given me so many ideas!

妳的文章給了我很多點子！

9 →

He preached the ball and the batter hit it.

他投球出去，打擊者打到了球。

10 →

I figured out the best method to clam all this information in my head in the shortest time possible.

我想出用最短時間讀完這一大堆資料的最佳方法。

11 →

She baked clamps and served them for dinner.

她烤蛤蜊當晚餐。

12 →

She's the first female president.

她是第一位女總統。

13 →

The part is cramped to the machine.

那個零件被夾在機器上。

❶ presented

❷ cramp

❸ itch

❹ reached

❺ residents

❻ article

❼ president

❽ ○

❾ preached → pitched

❿ clam → cram

⓫ clamps → clams

⓬ ○

⓭ cramped → clamped

加碼字母

+R

試試看

把左邊的字加一個*r*，會變成什麼字？

age	變老	*r*age	
cop	警察	c*r*op	
gem	寶石	ge*r*m	
oar	槳	*r*oar	
tap	輕拍	t*r*ap	
beak	鳥嘴	b*r*eak	
bust	半身像	bu*r*st	
camp	營地	c*r*amp	

試試看

把右邊的字減一個*r*，會變成什麼字？

cane	c*r*ane	鶴
chip	chi*r*p	鳥鳴
cook	c*r*ook	彎曲
dead	d*r*ead	可怕的
emit	*r*emit	匯款
font	f*r*ont	前面
gape	g*r*ape	葡萄
gaze	g*r*aze	吃草

試試看

把左邊的字加一個*r*，會變成什麼字？

kill	殺死	→	**k*r*ill**
tend	傾向	→	**t*r*end**
tuck	塞進	→	**t*r*uck**
anger	生氣	→	***r*anger**
couch	長沙發	→	**c*r*ouch**
sauce	調味醬	→	**sauce*r***
singe	烤焦	→	**singe*r***
spout	噴出	→	**sp*r*out**

試試看

把右邊的字減一個*r*，會變成什麼字？

stain	**st*r*ain** 拉緊
stand	**st*r*and** 擱淺
steak	**st*r*eak** 條紋
except	**exce*r*pt** 摘錄
galley	**galle*r*y** 走廊
contact	**cont*r*act** 契約
faction	**f*r*action** 片段
fiction	**f*r*iction** 摩擦

MP3-224

age
[edʒ]
動 變老

The young men aged quickly when they went to war.
這些年輕人參戰時老得很快。

cop
[kɑp]
名 警察

It's a cop and gangster movie.
這是一部警匪片。

gem
[dʒɛm]
名 寶石

She collects gems and makes jewellery.
她收集寶石做成珠寶首飾。

oar
[or]
名 槳

He made an oar out of some wood.
他用木頭做了一把槳。

tap
[tæp]
動 輕拍

Everyone was tapping their feet to the music.
大家都隨著音樂用腳打拍子。

beak
[bik]
名 鳥嘴

The crane has a long, sharp beak.
鶴有既長又尖的喙。

bust
[bʌst]
名 半身像

He has a bust of a former president in his office.
他的辦公室裡有前總統的半身像。

camp
[kæmp]
名 營地

The soldiers returned to their camp.
士兵回到他們的軍營。

rage
[redʒ]
動 肆虐

The typhoon is raging.
颱風正在肆虐。

crop
[krɑp]
名 作物

Rice is one of the most important crops.
稻米是最重要的農作物之一。

germ
[dʒɝm]
名 細菌

There are probably many germs on the floor in this room.
房間的地板上也許有很多細菌。

roar
[ror]
動 吼叫

My boss roared with anger.
我的老闆氣得大叫。

trap
[træp]
動 使落入圈套

I was trapped in the traffic jam.
我被困在車陣中。

break
[brek]
名 休息

Let's take a break.
我們休息一下吧。

burst
[bɝst]
動 爆發

The tire suddenly burst.
輪胎突然就爆了。

cramp
[kræmp]
名 抽筋

She got a cramp when she was jogging.
她慢跑時抽筋了。

MP3-225

cane
[ken]
名 手杖，拐杖

He made a cane out of a piece of wood.
他用一塊木頭做出一支手杖。

chip
[tʃɪp]
動 在⋯上造成缺口

I fell down and chipped my tooth.
我跌了一跤，牙齒撞缺了一角。

cook
[kʊk]
動 煮

Good seasonings are the key to good cooking.
好的調味料是做好菜的關鍵。

dead
[dɛd]
形 死的

We saw a dead rat in the garden.
我們在花園裡看到一隻死老鼠。

emit
[ɪˋmɪt]
動 發出

The machine emits a beeping sound when the battery is low.
電池電量不足時，那台機器會發出嗶嗶聲。

font
[fɑnt]
名 字型

This program has over fifty fonts.
這個程式有超過五十種字型。

gape
[gep]
動 目瞪口呆

They stood gaping at the unimaginable scene.
他們站著呆望著這副難以想像的景象。

gaze
[gez]
動 凝視

The policeman gazed at the dark corner in the distance.
警察注視著遠方漆黑的角落。

crane
[kren]
名 鶴

A crane flew off into the sunset.
一隻鶴飛進入夕陽餘暉之中。

chirp
[tʃɝp]
動 鳥鳴

We heard the birds chirping in the tree.
我們聽見小鳥在樹上啾啾叫。

crook
[krʊk]
動 彎曲

There's a crook in the river ahead.
前方的河道有一個轉彎處。

dread
[drɛd]
形 可怕的

I'm filled with dread thinking about the meeting tonight.
想到今晚的會議，我就充滿可怕的念頭。

remit
[rɪˋmɪt]
動 匯款

Please remit the money at once.
請立刻匯款。

front
[frʌnt]
名 前面

He always sits in the front of the classroom.
他總是坐在教室的前方。

grape
[grep]
名 葡萄

Wine is made from grapes.
葡萄酒是葡萄製成的。

graze
[grez]
動 吃草

The cows grazed in the field all day.
母牛整天都在原野上吃草。

MP3-226

kill
[kɪl]
動 殺死

She killed the mosquito by hitting it with her hand.
她用手打死蚊子。

tend
[tɛnd]
動 傾向

This car tends to drift to the right.
這輛車會往右偏。

tuck
[tʌk]
動 把…塞進

Tuck your shirt into your pants.
把你的襯衫紮進褲子裡。

anger
[`æŋgɚ]
名 生氣

Her anger caused her to say some bad things.
她的憤怒使她出言不遜。

couch
[kaʊtʃ]
名 長沙發

This couch folds out into a bed.
這張沙發椅展開來就變成一張床。

sauce
[sɔs]
名 調味醬

This spaghetti sauce is delicious.
這個義大利麵醬味道很好。

singe
[sɪndʒ]
動 烤焦

She singed the steak in a frying pan.
她用煎鍋把牛排煎焦了。

spout
[spaʊt]
動 噴出

Water spouted out of a hole in the pipe.
水從水管上的一個洞噴出來。

krill
[krɪl]
名 磷蝦

The whale eats only krill.
鯨只吃磷蝦。

trend
[trɛnd]
名 趨勢

The fashion trend changes tremendously.
時尚趨勢的變化很大。

truck
[trʌk]
名 卡車

This company uses trucks to deliver its products to various stores.
這家公司用卡車把產品運送到各家店。

ranger
[`rendʒɚ]
名 國家公園管理員

Jeff works as a ranger in a park.
傑夫在公園中擔任管理員。

crouch
[krautʃ]
動 蹲伏

The tiger crouched and waited for the deer to come closer.
老虎蹲下埋伏，等待鹿靠近。

saucer
[`sɔsɚ]
名 淺碟

You can put soy sauce in your saucer.
你可以把醬油倒在淺碟子裡。

singer
[`sɪŋɚ]
名 歌手

The singer began her career as an actress.
這個歌手是以女演員發跡。

sprout
[spraut]
動 發芽

The seeds you planted will sprout in a week or two.
你種的種子會在一、兩週內發芽。

MP3-227

stain
[sten]
動 沾污

The tomato juice fell and stained her white shirt.
番茄汁打翻，弄髒了她的白襯衫。

stand
[stænd]
動 站立

Will you stand up now?
可以請你現在站起來嗎？

steak
[stek]
名 牛排

This restaurant is famous for its steaks and salads.
這家餐廳以牛排和沙拉聞名。

except
[ɪk`sɛpt]
介 除…之外

Except for the cake, we have no other dessert.
除了蛋糕，我們沒有別的甜點了。

galley
[`gælɪ]
名 廚房

They prepared their dinner in the ship's galley.
他們在船上的廚房準備晚餐。

contact
[`kɑntækt]
名 接觸

I haven't made contact with him for a long time.
我已經好久沒跟他聯絡了。

faction
[`fækʃən]
名 派別

This party has split into two factions.
這個政黨已經分裂成兩派。

fiction
[`fɪkʃən]
名 小說

That book in the fiction section is increasingly popular.
小說區的那本書越來越熱門。

strain
[stren]
動 拉緊

The rope was strained under the heavy load.
沈重的貨物下有用一條繩子綁得很緊。

strand
[strænd]
動 擱淺

They were stranded on an island when their boat broke.
他們的船故障時，他們擱淺在一座島上。

streak
[strik]
名 條紋

Your makeup left streaks on your face.
你臉上的妝有些沒抹勻的痕跡。

excerpt
[`ɛksɜpt]
名 摘錄

Here is an excerpt from the new book.
這是一份那本新書的摘錄。

gallery
[`gælərɪ]
名 畫廊

Her paintings are displayed in the gallery.
她的畫正在畫廊裡展示。

contract
[`kɑntrækt]
名 契約

They signed a contract to rent a flat.
他們簽約租了一個公寓。

fraction
[`frækʃən]
名 片段

A fraction is any portion of a whole.
片段是指全體的任一部分。

friction
[`frɪkʃən]
名 摩擦

Friction caused the wheels to get hot.
摩擦使輪胎發熱。

想想看 要將填入的字改為合乎文法的形式喔！

下面這些句子少了哪個字？

except	*age*
couch	*crop*
tap	*break*
germ	*front*

1. **We'll take a _______ as soon as we clean this room.**
   我們房間一掃乾淨就來休息一下。

2. **There is a big tree in _______ of my house.**
   我家前面有棵大樹。

3. **The farmers had some _______ ruined by the dry summer.**
   農民的部分作物因為夏季乾旱枯死。

4. **Some people seem to _______ faster than others.**
   有些人好像老得比較快。

5. **She washed her hands to kill any _______.**
   她清洗雙手以殺死所有細菌。

6. **The boy is lying on the _______.**
   男孩躺在長沙發上。

7. **All the students failed the exam _______ Kelly.**
   除了凱莉，所有學生都沒通過考試。

找找看

以下句子在前面都出現過，你確定都讀熟了嗎？
找找看下面的句子有沒有拼錯的字。
錯字訂正於上方箭頭處，沒錯字請打“○”

下面哪些句子有字拼錯了？

8 →

That book in the friction section is increasingly popular.

小說區的那本書越來越熱門。

9 →

They signed a contact to rent a flat.

他們簽約租了一個公寓。

10 →

Water sprouted out of a hole in the pipe.

水從水管上的一個洞噴出來。

11 →

He made a crane out of a piece of wood.

他用一塊木頭做成一支拐杖。

12 →

The fashion tend changes tremendously.

時尚趨勢的變化很大。

13 →

She singed the steak in a frying pan.

她用煎鍋把牛排煎焦了。

1. break
2. front
3. crops
4. age
5. germs
6. couch
7. except
8. friction → fiction
9. contact → contract
10. sprouted → spouted
11. crane → cane
12. tend → trend
13. ○

加碼字母 +S

試試看

把左邊的字加一個*s*，會變成什麼字？

age	年齡	→	***s*age**	
lap	膝部	→	***s*lap**	
oak	橡樹	→	***s*oak**	
oar	槳	→	***s*oar**	
out	出外	→	**ou*s*t**	
pan	平底鍋	→	***s*pan**	
wan	黯淡的	→	***s*wan**	
way	路途，路線	→	***s*way**	

試試看

把右邊的字減一個*s*，會變成什麼字？

boat	boa*s*t	吹噓
boot	boo*s*t	增加
corn	*s*corn	藐視
ever	*s*ever	切斷
hare	*s*hare	分享
harp	*s*harp	尖的
pace	*s*pace	空間
palm	p*s*alm	讚美詩

試試看

把左邊的字加一個*s*，會變成什麼字？

park	公園	→	***s*park**
root	根	→	**roo*s*t**
take	拿	→	***s*take**
tale	傳說	→	***s*tale**
trap	困住	→	***s*trap**
tray	托盤	→	***s*tray**
trip	旅行	→	***s*trip**
warm	溫暖的	→	***s*warm**

試試看

把右邊的字減一個*s*，會變成什麼字？

well	→	***s*well** 膨脹
wing	→	***s*wing** 搖擺
wipe	→	***s*wipe** 刷卡
ample	→	***s*ample** 例子
comic	→	**co*s*mic** 宇宙的
train	→	***s*train** 沈動壓力
trait	→	***s*trait** 海峽
witch	→	***s*witch** 切換開關

MP3-228

age
[edʒ]
名 年齡

I need to know your age and your full name.
我需要知道你的年紀和全名。

lap
[læp]
名 膝部

She placed the child in her lap.
她把孩子放在膝上。

oak
[ok]
名 橡樹

This desk is made from real oak.
這張書桌是用橡木實木做的。

oar
[or]
名 槳

He hit the water with an oar to splash his friend.
他用槳打水,潑水在朋友身上。

out
[aʊt]
副 出外

I'll be out of town this weekend.
我這個週末會出遠門。

pan
[pæn]
名 平底鍋

She made bacon and eggs in the new pan I gave her.
她用我送她的新平底鍋煎培根和雞蛋。

wan
[wɑn]
形 黯淡的

His wan smile concerned me.
他黯淡無奈的笑容令我擔心。

way
[we]
名 路途,路線

Can you show me the way to the airport?
你可以告訴我去機場要怎麼走嗎?

sage
[sedʒ]
名 聖人

The sage makes predictions about the future.
聖人對未來做出預測。

slap
[slæp]
動 打耳光

She slapped her boyfriend when he said something bad.
她男朋友說了些不該說的話時，她打了他一巴掌。

soak
[sok]
動 浸泡

I'm going to Yangmingshan to soak in the hot springs.
我要去陽明山泡溫泉。

soar
[sor]
動 翱翔

The airplane soared high above the clouds.
飛機在雲層上方高處翱翔。

oust
[aust]
動 驅逐

The man was ousted from office.
那個男子被逐出辦公室。

span
[spæn]
名 一段時間

I was in the Army for a long span of time.
我曾在軍中很長一段時間。

swan
[swan]
名 天鵝

Swans sail on the lake gracefully.
天鵝在湖面優雅地划水前進。

sway
[swe]
動 搖動

The tree swayed slowly in the wind.
這棵樹在風中緩緩搖擺。

MP3-229

boat
[bot]
名 小船

We're in the same boat. I am running out of money, too.
我們同病相憐。我也快要沒錢了。

boot
[bʊt]
名 靴

She has a pair of boots in her car.
她在她車上放了一雙靴子。

corn
[kɔrn]
名 玉米

Corn soup is my favorite soup.
玉米湯是我最喜歡的湯。

ever
[ˋɛvɚ]
副 在任何時候

She's the prettiest girl I've ever seen.
她是我見過最漂亮的女孩。

hare
[hɛr]
名 野兔

The eagle caught a hare and ate it.
老鷹抓住野兔並把牠吃掉。

harp
[hɑrp]
名 豎琴

She plays the harp very well.
她豎琴彈得很好。

pace
[pes]
動 慢慢地走

He paced around the room while thinking about the problem.
他緩緩地邊繞著房間走，一邊思考那個問題。

palm
[pɑm]
名 手掌

Palm readers get their information from the lines on your hands.
手相師從你的掌紋讀出訊息。

boast
[bost]
動 吹嘘

She boasts a lot about how much money her father makes.
她很愛吹噓她爸爸賺了多少錢。

boost
[bust]
動 增加

Did Bush's visit to Britain boost his popularity?
布希訪問英國有提高他的人氣嗎？

scorn
[skɔrn]
動 藐視

She was scorned after she angered her friends.
她讓朋友發脾氣之後，朋友都不理她。

sever
[ˋsɛvɚ]
動 切斷

The wire was severed.
電線被切斷了。

share
[ʃɑr]
動 分享

This driveway is shared by us and our neighbors.
這條車道是由我們及鄰居共有。

sharp
[ʃɑrp]
形 尖的

The chef's knife was very sharp.
廚師的刀子很利。

space
[spes]
名 空間

There's not enough space to add an extra desk here.
這裡沒有足夠空間再放一張書桌。

psalm
[sɑm]
名 讚美詩

This is a psalm from the Bible.
這是取自聖經的一首讚美詩。

MP3-230

park
[pɑrk]
名 公園

This site is where the new city park will be built.
這個地點就是要興建新市鎮公園的地方。

root
[rut]
名 根

The roots of his hair are black, but the rest is blonde.
他的髮根是黑色的，但其他部分都是金色的。

take
[tek]
動 拿

She took the wrong luggage.
她拿錯行李了。

tale
[tel]
名 傳說

A tale is just a kind of short story.
傳說只是一種短篇故事。

trap
[træp]
動 困住

We were trapped in the elevator when the power went out.
停電時我們被困在電梯裡。

tray
[tre]
名 托盤

She carried the drinks to the guests using a tray.
她用托盤把飲料送去給客人。

trip
[trɪp]
名 旅行

I'd like to take a trip to Egypt this winter.
今年冬天我想去埃及旅行。

warm
[wɔrm]
形 溫暖的

This jacket looks warm.
這件夾克看起來很保暖。

spark
[spɑrk]
名 火花

A little spark kindles a great fire.
星星之火，可以燎原。

roost
[rust]
名 鳥巢

The bird built a roost in the tree.
鳥在樹上造了一個鳥巢。

stake
[stek]
名 樁

This stake is holding up the tent.
這支樁撐起了帳篷。

stale
[stel]
形 不新鮮的

The cheese is getting stale.
起司不新鮮了。

strap
[stræp]
名 吊環

Hold onto the strap so you don't fall down.
握住這個吊環才不會摔倒。

stray
[stre]
形 走失的，零星的

You've got a few stray hairs hanging down.
你這兒垂下幾根沒綁到的頭髮。

strip
[strɪp]
名 細長紙片

He wrote my name on a strip of paper.
他把我的名字寫在一張紙條上。

swarm
[swɔrm]
動 成群地移動

The bees swarmed around the bear.
蜜蜂成群圍繞著熊。

MP3-231

well
[wɛl]
副 很好地

My sister plays the piano very well.
我姊姊彈鋼琴彈得很好。

wing
[wɪŋ]
名 翅膀

That bird can't fly because someone has clipped its wings.
那隻鳥不能飛，因為有人把牠的翅膀剪斷了。

wipe
[waɪp]
動 擦去

Please wipe the water off the table.
請擦乾桌上的水。

ample
[`æmpḷ]
形 充裕的

We have ample supplies for the outing.
我們有充裕的補給品可供出外郊遊使用。

comic
[`kɑmɪk]
形 滑稽的

The teacher's comic antics made all of the students laugh.
老師喜感逗趣的動作把所有學生都逗笑了。

train
[tren]
名 火車

She goes to work by train every day.
她每天搭火車去上班。

trait
[tret]
名 特點

What special traits does this have?
這有什麼特點?

witch
[wɪtʃ]
名 巫婆

The witch lives alone with a black cat.
這個獨居的女巫養了一隻黑貓。

swell
[swɛl]
動 膨脹

Joseph's left foot began to swell after being hit by the bike.
喬瑟夫的左腳被腳踏車撞到之後腫了起來。

swing
[swɪŋ]
動 搖擺

The children swung from the rope and jumped into the water.
孩子們從繩子盪下來跳進水裡。

swipe
[swaɪp]
動 刷卡

They swiped my card twice!
他們拿我的卡刷了兩次！

sample
[`sæmpl]
名 例子

Here is a sample of my work.
這是一份我的作品實例。

cosmic
[`kɑzmɪk]
形 宇宙的

Cosmic distances are too large to imagine.
宇宙間的距離大到無法想像。

strain
[stren]
名 沈重壓力

There's a lot of strain on this board here.
這個木板承受很沉重的壓力。

strait
[stret]
名 海峽

The boats had a race through the narrow strait.
幾艘船通過狹窄的海峽進行一場競賽。

switch
[swɪtʃ]
動 切換開關

Could you switch off the light?
你可以把燈關掉嗎？

想想看 要將填入的字改為合乎文法的形式喔！

下面這些句子少了哪個字？

slap	*sharp*
share	*space*
park	*root*
way	*strip*

1. **May I _______ this cake with you?**
我可以和你分享這個蛋糕嗎？

2. **Some _______ of plants can be eaten.**
有些植物的根可以吃。

3. **Every time I _______ at a fly, it flies away.**
每次我打蒼蠅，牠都飛走。

4. **Use these _______ of cloth to tie the package.**
用這些長條的布來綁包裹。

5. **This knife is very _______.**
那把刀很利。

6. **There is a huge _______ in the middle of the school.**
學校中央有很大的空地。

7. **Joey and Chris are passing a football in the _______.**
喬依和克利斯在公園傳接橄欖球。

以下句子在前面都出現過，你確定都讀熟了嗎？
找找看下面的句子有沒有拼錯的字。
錯字訂正於上方箭頭處，沒錯字請打“○”

下面哪些句子有字拼錯了？

8 →

She placed the child in her slap.

她把孩子放在膝上。

9 →

The teacher's cosmic antics made all of the students laugh.

老師喜感逗趣的動作把所有學生都逗笑了。

10 →

Could you swich off the light?

你可以把燈關掉嗎？

11 →

She took the wrong luggage.

她拿錯行李了。

12 →

Hold onto the strip so you don't fall down.

握住這個吊環才不會摔倒。

13 →

They swinged my card twice!

他們拿我的卡刷了兩次！

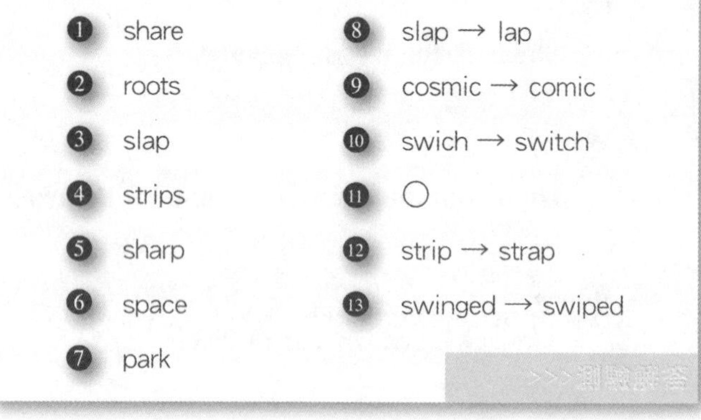

1. share
2. roots
3. slap
4. strips
5. sharp
6. space
7. park
8. slap → lap
9. cosmic → comic
10. swich → switch
11. ○
12. strip → strap
13. swinged → swiped

>>>測驗解答

加碼字母 +T

試試看

把左邊的字加一個*t*，會變成什麼字？

ram	公羊	→	***t*ram**	
rap	拍擊	→	***t*rap**	
rim	邊緣	→	***t*rim**	
sir	先生	→	**s*t*ir**	
come	來	→	**come*t***	
ease	緩和	→	***t*ease**	
flee	逃走	→	**flee*t***	
high	高的	→	***t*high**	

試試看

把右邊的字減一個*t*，會變成什麼字？

horn	***t*horn**	刺
race	***t*race**	描繪
rail	***t*rail**	小道
rash	***t*rash**	垃圾
seed	**s*t*eed**	駿馬
sink	**s*t*ink**	發臭
error	***t*error**	驚駭
issue	***t*issue**	面紙

MP3-232

ram
[ræm]
名 公羊

That ram is very large and it looks angry.
那隻公羊很大，而且看起來很生氣。

rap
[ræp]
動 拍擊

She rapped the window to get my attention.
她拍窗吸引我的注意。

rim
[rɪm]
名 邊緣

They camped in a tent at the rim of a canyon.
他們在峽谷邊紮帳篷露營。

sir
[sɜ]
名 先生

How may I help you, sir?
先生，有什麼我能效勞的嗎？

come
[kʌm]
動 來

My new co-worker comes to work late every day.
我的新同事每天上班都遲到。

ease
[iz]
動 緩和

Don't try so hard, just ease into it.
別這麼用力，輕一點。

flee
[fli]
動 逃走

All the gangsters fled when the police came.
警方來的時候，盜匪全跑光了。

high
[haɪ]
形 高的

I can't reach the top; it's too high for me.
我搆不到最上面，那對我來說太高了。

tram
[træm]
名 有軌電車

This tram runs in a circle around the small town.
這輛有軌電車環繞小鎮行駛。

trap
[træp]
名 陷阱

The rabbit was caught in a trap I made.
兔子被我做的陷阱困住了。

trim
[trɪm]
名 修剪（頭髮）

It's been a month since I got a trim.
我上次修剪頭髮到現在已經過了一個月。

stir
[stɜ]
動 攪動

Mother stirred the eggs with the flour.
媽媽把雞蛋和麵粉攪拌在一起。

comet
[ˋkɑmɪt]
名 彗星

Did you see the comet in the sky last night?
你昨晚有看到天上那顆彗星嗎？

tease
[tiz]
動 取笑

Don't tease these kids.
別捉弄這些小孩子。

fleet
[flit]
名 艦隊

The fleet has moved to the Persian Gulf.
艦隊已經移師到波斯灣。

thigh
[θaɪ]
名 大腿

I'm tired of looking at these thunder thighs.
我受不了再繼續看到我的超級象腿了。

MP3-233

horn
[horn]
名 角

That bull has very sharp horns—be careful.
那頭公牛的角很尖——要小心。

race
[res]
名 種族

The human race has a very long history.
人類有長久的歷史。

rail
[rel]
名 鐵軌

This special train only uses one rail.
這輛特殊的火車只在單軌上行駛。

rash
[ræʃ]
形 輕率的

She made a rash decision when she was angry.
她生氣時做了一個輕率的決定。

seed
[sid]
名 種子

She bought tomato seeds to plant in her garden.
她買了番茄種子要種在花園裡。

sink
[sɪŋk]
名 水槽

There are many cups in the sink.
水槽裡有很多個杯子。

error
[`ɛrɚ]
名 錯誤

She made an error on her test.
她在考試時犯了個錯誤。

issue
[`ɪʃu]
動 核發

The company just issued new uniforms to everyone — did you get yours yet?
公司剛剛發了新制服給大家——你拿到了嗎？

thorn
[θorn]
名 刺

Be careful of the thorns on this rose.
小心這朵玫瑰上的刺。

trace
[tres]
動 描繪

The children traced their hands onto paper.
這些孩童把他們的手描在紙上。

trail
[trel]
名 小道

We walked on the trail between the ocean and the hills.
我們走在山海之間的小徑上。

trash
[træʃ]
名 垃圾

After the hurricane, trash was scattered everywhere.
颶風之後，到處都是垃圾。

steed
[stid]
名 駿馬

The cowboy wrote a poem about his steed.
牛仔寫了一首有關他駿馬的詩。

stink
[stɪŋk]
動 發臭

This bug spray stinks!
這種殺蟲劑好臭！

terror
[ˋtɛrɚ]
名 驚駭

I am in terror of the mean dog which bit me once.
我很怕那隻咬過我的惡犬。

tissue
[ˋtɪʃʊ]
名 面紙

The bathroom is out of tissues.
廁所裡沒有衛生紙了。

想想看 要將填入的字改為合乎文法的形式喔！

下面這些句子少了哪個字？

sink	*tease*
stink	*trap*
thigh	*tissue*
trail	*issue*

1. **We had to clear the _______ after the windy night.**
颳了一夜的風之後，我們得去把小徑清理乾淨。

2. **We didn't know what to do when a tiger fell into our _______.**
一隻老虎跑進我們設下的陷阱時，我們完全不知所措。

3. **The _______ is full of dirty dishes.**
水槽裡堆滿髒碗盤。

4. **The country will _______ new ID cards next year.**
國家明年會核發新版身分證。

5. **She _______ her friend about losing the contest.**
她嘲笑朋友比賽落敗。

6. **Something in the kitchen really _______.**
廚房裡不知有什麼東西好臭。

7. **Could you please hand me a _______ from the table?**
麻煩你從桌上拿一張面紙給我好嗎？

找找看

以下句子在前面都出現過，你確定都讀熟了嗎？
找找看下面的句子有沒有拼錯的字。
錯字訂正於上方箭頭處，沒錯字請打“○”

下面哪些句子有字拼錯了？

⑧ →

Did you see the comet in the sky last night?

你昨晚有看到天上那顆彗星嗎？

⑨ →

Be careful of the horns on this rose.

小心這朵玫瑰上的刺。

⑩ →

She raped the window to get my attention.

她拍窗吸引我的注意。

⑪ →

Don't tissue these kids.

別捉弄這些小孩子。

⑫ →

The rabbit was caught in a trim I made.

兔子被我做的陷阱困住了。

⑬ →

All the gangsters fleet when the police came.

警方來的時候，盜匪全跑光了。

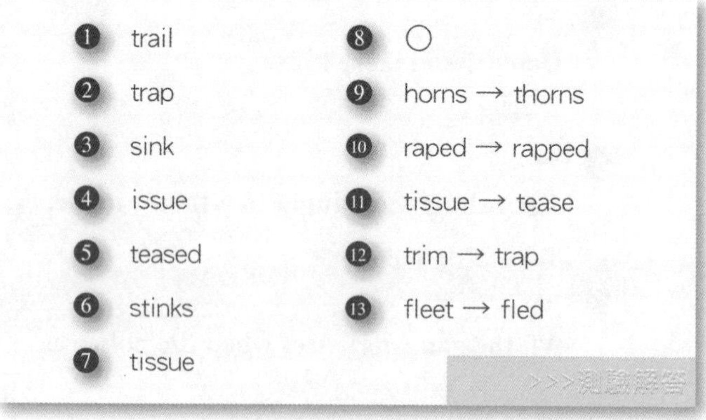

1. trail
2. trap
3. sink
4. issue
5. teased
6. stinks
7. tissue
8. ○
9. horns → thorns
10. raped → rapped
11. tissue → tease
12. trim → trap
13. fleet → fled

>>>測驗解答

加碼字母 +U

試試看

把左邊的字加一個*u*，會變成什麼字？

boy	男孩	→	**b*u*oy**
cop	警察	→	**co*u*p**
bond	結合力	→	**bo*u*nd**
form	形成	→	**for*u*m**
morn	早晨	→	**mo*u*rn**
rose	玫瑰花	→	**ro*u*se**
sage	賢明的	→	***u*sage**
vale	溪谷	→	**val*u*e**

MP3-234

boy
[bɔɪ]
名 男孩

That man is forty years old but still acts like a little boy.
那個男人已經四十歲了，但行為還像個小男孩。

cop
[kɑp]
名 警察

The cops always give about a ten-mile-per-hour margin before they ticket you.
警察開罰單之前，都有給予時速十英里的通融範圍。

bond
[bɑnd]
名 結合力

The bond between the pieces is very strong.
這兩塊東西之間的黏力很強。

form
[fɔrm]
動 形成

The parade formed a beautiful pattern.
遊行隊伍排成一個漂亮的圖案。

morn
[mɔrn]
名 早晨

Early in the morn the rooster crows.
公雞在清晨鳴叫。

rose
[roz]
名 玫瑰花

Some people say that roses are difficult to grow.
有人說玫瑰很難種。

sage
[sedʒ]
形 賢明的

Her sage advice saved hundreds of lives.
她睿智的建議救了數百條生命。

vale
[vel]
名 溪谷

His house is located in a large vale.
他家位在一個廣大的溪谷裡。

buoy
[bɔɪ]
名 浮標

They tied their boat to a buoy in the bay.
他們把船繫在港邊的一個浮筒上。

coup
[ku]
名 政變

The president lost power because of a coup.
這個總統因為政變而失勢。

bound
[baʊnd]
形 正在前往的

The travelers are bound for Caracas.
這些遊客正前往卡拉卡斯。

forum
[`forəm]
名 討論會

We'd like to hold a forum to discuss these issues more.
我們想要舉辦一場論壇來多進一步討論這些問題。

mourn
[morn]
動 哀悼

The people wore black to mourn their father.
他們穿黑色衣服為他們的父親服喪。

rouse
[raʊz]
動 喚起

They roused up some supporters to attend the protest.
他們鼓動部分支持者參加抗議。

usage
[`jusɪdʒ]
名 用法

The usage of fresh herbs in our cooking is a family tradition.
做菜時使用新鮮香料是我們家的傳統。

value
[`vælju]
名 價值

The value of the cars will drop at the end of this year.
車子的價格將於年底下跌。

想想看 要將填入的字改為合乎文法的形式喔！

下面這些句子少了哪個字？

rouse	*cop*
form	*forum*
mourn	*bond*
usage	*bound*

❶ **They made an online _______ to discuss their hobby.**
他們開了一個線上討論區談論他們的嗜好。

❷ **This pot is _______ from a special kind of clay.**
那個鍋子是用一種特殊陶土製成的。

❸ **It seems the candidate is _______ for the office of senator.**
這個候選人似乎篤定能進入參議院。

❹ **The soldiers were _______ when their leader made an announcement.**
士兵被全部叫醒，起來聽長官宣布消息。

❺ **This book will teach you the proper _______ of certain idioms.**
這本書會教你一些成語的正確用法。

❻ **They _______ the death of their father for several months.**
他們為父親去世哀悼了好幾個月。

❼ **The _______ told me I shouldn't drive so fast.**
警察跟我說我不該開快車。

找找看

以下句子在前面都出現過，你確定都讀熟了嗎？
找找看下面的句子有沒有拼錯的字。
錯字訂正於上方箭頭處，沒錯字請打“○”

下面哪些句子有字拼錯了？

8 →

The vale of the cars will drop at the end of this year.

車子的價格將於年底下跌

9 →

The travelers are bound for Caracas.

這些遊客正前往卡拉卡斯。

10 →

We'd like to hold a form to discuss these issues more.

我們想要舉辦一場論壇來多進一步討論這些問題。

11 →

The parade forumed a beautiful pattern.

遊行隊伍排成一個漂亮的圖案。

12 →

The bound between the pieces is very strong.

這兩塊東西之間的黏力很強。

13 →

The usage of fresh herbs in our cooking is a family tradition.

做菜時使用新鮮香料是我們家的傳統。

1. forum
2. formed
3. bound
4. roused
5. usage
6. mourned
7. cop
8. vale → value
9. ○
10. form → forum
11. forumed → formed
12. bound → bond
13. ○

加碼字母

+W

試試看

把左邊的字加一個*w*，會變成什麼字？

age	時代	→	***w*age**
and	及	→	***w*and**
art	美術	→	***w*art**
hip	臀部	→	***w*hip**
vie	競爭	→	**vie*w***
hale	健壯的	→	***w*hale**
helm	舵	→	***w*helm**
help	幫助	→	***w*help**

MP3-235

age
[edʒ]
名 時代

This story is set in a long ago age.
這個故事的時代背景設定在很久以前的時代。

and
[ænd]
連 及

Your driving was reckless and unsafe.
你車開得毫無章法又不安全。

art
[ɑrt]
名 美術

This art class will teach you how to paint and draw.
這堂美術課將會教你如何畫畫。

hip
[hɪp]
名 臀部，髖部

She measured her hips before shopping for the dress.
她在買洋裝前先測量她的臀圍。

vie
[vaɪ]
動 競爭

The two companies vied for the government contract.
兩家公司相互爭奪這份政府合約。

hale
[hel]
形 健壯的（極少用）

He's a hale and hearty man.
他是個健壯的大塊頭。

helm
[hɛlm]
名 舵

The helm of this boat is made of wood.
這艘船的舵是木製的。

help
[hɛlp]
名 幫助

She helped her mother clean the house.
她幫媽媽打掃房子。

wage
[wedʒ]
名 報酬

My company pays double wages for overtime hours.
我們公司付的加班費是時薪加倍。

wand
[wɑnd]
名 魔杖

The magician uses a black and white wand.
魔術師使用一支黑白相間的魔杖。

wart
[wɔrt]
名 疣

The boy has a wart on his thumb.
男孩的拇指上有一個疣。

whip
[hwɪp]
名 鞭子

There is a whip on the horse cart.
馬拉的貨車上有一條鞭子。

view
[vju]
名 景色

The view of Hong Kong at night is great.
香港的夜景很棒。

whale
[wel]
名 鯨

The whale traveled from Alaska to Hawaii with its new baby.
鯨帶著牠的新生兒從阿拉斯加游到夏威夷。

whelm
[hwɛlm]
動 壓倒

The word whelm has been replaced by the words overwhelm and underwhelm.
whelm這個字已經被overwhelm和underwhelm所取代。

whelp
[hwɛlp]
名 小狗

There are three whelps in this litter.
這個垃圾堆裡有三隻小狗。

想想看 要將填入的字改為合乎文法的形式喔！

下面這些句子少了哪個字？

wage	*age*
view	*help*
wand	*hip*
whale	*art*

1. **You can see _______ swimming off the coast of Maine.**
在緬因州外海可以看見鯨悠游。

2. **They took pictures of the beautiful _______ from atop the mountain.**
他們拍下從山頂鳥瞰的美景照片。

3. **He tied the rope to his _______ and began pulling the boxes.**
他把繩子綁在臀部，開始拖行那些箱子。

4. **She studied _______ in school and now works at a museum.**
她在學校念的是藝術，目前在博物館工作。

5. **People say we're living in the _______ of the computer now.**
大家都說我們現在身處於電腦時代。

6. **He asked his teacher for _______ on the difficult problem.**
他請老師幫他解決困難的問題。

7. **The magician used a _______ to make smoke and fire.**
魔術師用一根魔杖變出煙和火。

找找看

以下句子在前面都出現過，你確定都讀熟了嗎？
找找看下面的句子有沒有拼錯的字。
錯字訂正於上方箭頭處，沒錯字請打“○”

下面哪些句子有字拼錯了？

⑧ →

This art class will teach you how to paint and draw.

這堂美術課將會教你如何畫畫。

⑨ →

The magician uses a black and white whip.

魔術師使用一支黑白相間的魔杖。

⑩ →

The whale traveled from Alaska to Hawaii with its new baby.

鯨帶著牠的新生寶寶從阿拉斯加游到夏威夷。

⑪ →

The boy has a ward on his thumb.

男孩的拇指上有一個疣。

⑫ →

She measured her hip before shopping for the dress.

她在買洋裝前先測量她的臀圍。

⑬ →

My company pays double warts for overtime hours.

我們公司付的加班費是時薪加倍。

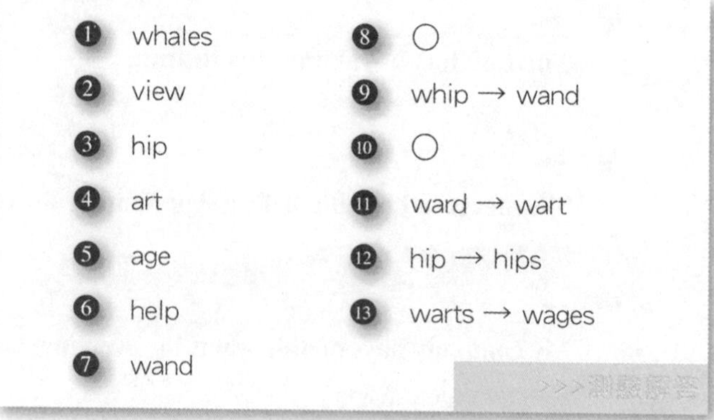

1. whales
2. view
3. hip
4. art
5. age
6. help
7. wand
8. ○
9. whip → wand
10. ○
11. ward → wart
12. hip → hips
13. warts → wages

>>>測驗解答

加碼字母 +Y

試試看

把左邊的字加一個*y*，會變成什麼字？

tin	錫	→	**tin*y***
boot	戰利品	→	**boot*y***
bull	公牛	→	**bull*y***
iron	鐵	→	**iron*y***
wear	戴著	→	**wear*y***
colon	冒號	→	**colon*y***
miser	守財奴	→	**miser*y***
treat	請客	→	**treat*y***

MP3-236

tin

[tɪn]

名 錫

This small cup is made from tin.

這個小杯子是錫做的。

boot

[but]

名 靴子

Carrie likes to wear boots in the winter.

凱莉冬天喜歡穿靴子。

bull

[bʊl]

名 公牛

The bull got angry and ran away.

這頭公牛生氣跑走了。

iron

[`aɪɚn]

名 鐵

The old boat is made of iron.

這艘老舊的船是鐵製的。

wear

[wɛr]

動 穿戴

She decided to wear her school uniform to the meeting after school.

她決定放學後要穿著學校制服去開會。

colon

[`kolən]

名 冒號

This sentence should have a colon.

這個句子應該要有個冒號。

miser

[`maɪzɚ]

名 守財奴

The miser is not liked by anyone.

沒有人喜歡這個守財奴。

treat

[trit]

動 請客

I'd like to treat you to dinner when you have time.

你有空的時候，我想請你吃晚飯。

tiny
[ˋtaɪnɪ]
形 極小的

Fleas are tiny pests.
跳蚤是很小隻的害蟲。

booty
[ˋbutɪ]
名 戰利品

Oil is the booty of the war in the desert.
原油是這場沙漠戰爭中的戰利品。

bully
[ˋbulɪ]
名 惡霸

Joe got beat up by a bully at his school.
喬在學校被一個流氓揍。

irony
[ˋaɪrənɪ]
名 諷刺

The irony is that although she is a vegetarian, she works as a chef in a steakhouse.
諷刺的是她雖然吃素，卻在牛排館當主廚。

weary
[ˋwɪrɪ]
形 疲倦的

The weary man fell asleep quickly.
這名疲倦的男子很快就睡著了。

colony
[ˋkɑlənɪ]
名 殖民地

Vietnam used to be a French colony.
越南曾經是法國殖民地。

misery
[ˋmɪzərɪ]
名 苦難

Grandmother has lived in misery since Grandfather passed away.
爺爺過世後，奶奶一直活在痛苦當中。

treaty
[ˋtritɪ]
名 條約

The two countries signed a treaty to end the war.
這兩個國家簽署條約來停止這場戰爭。

想想看 要將填入的字改為合乎文法的形式喔！

下面這些句子少了哪個字？

bully	*weary*
wear	*bull*
tiny	*colony*
misery	*wage*

1. **There is a small _______ of people on the tiny Pacific island.**
   那個太平洋小島上有一小群部落居民。

2. **He _______ his new hat when he went to the party.**
   他去參加派對時戴了一頂新帽子。

3. **This class has one very mean _______.**
   這個班上有一個很兇惡的流氓學生。

4. **We could see the _______ of the people in the photographs in the newspaper.**
   在報紙照片上可以看見人們所受的苦難。

5. **We are all tired and _______ after our long hike.**
   長途健行之後，我們都又累又倦。

6. **A _______ is often used before a list.**
   冒號經常在列舉清單前使用。

7. **Her hands are really _______.**
   她的手很細小。

以下句子在前面都出現過，你確定都讀熟了嗎？
找找看下面的句子有沒有拼錯的字。
錯字訂正於上方箭頭處，沒錯字請打“○”

下面哪些句子有字拼錯了？

8 →

Vietnam used to be a French colon.

越南曾經是法國殖民地。

9 →

Joe got beat up by bully at his school.

喬在學校被一個流氓揍。

10 →

Grandmother has lived in miser since Grandfather passed away.

爺爺過世後，奶奶一直活在痛苦當中。

11 →

The old boat is made of irony.

這艘老舊的船是鐵製的。

12 →

This sentence should have a clone.

這個句子應該要有個冒號。

13 →

Fleas are tinny pests.

跳蚤是微小的害蟲。

1. colony
2. wore
3. bully
4. misery
5. weary
6. colon
7. tiny
8. colon → colony
9. bully → a bully
10. miser → misery
11. irony → iron
12. clone → colon
13. tinny → tiny

>>>測驗解答

加碼字母

+其它

試試看

把左邊的字加上其它字母，會變成什麼字？

bar	桿子	→	**bar*k***
bun	小圓麵包	→	**bun*k***
clan	部落	→	**clan*k***
plan	計畫	→	**plan*k***
span	跨距	→	**span*k***
ice	冰	→	***v*ice**
navy	海軍	→	**na*v*vy**
omit	刪除	→	***v*omit**

MP3-237

bar
[bɑr]
名 桿子

The bar holding the baskets broke under the strain.
掛那幾個籃子的橫桿承受不住壓力而斷裂。

bun
[bʌn]
名 小圓麵包

They serve free buns before the steak.
上牛排前，他們提供免費的小麵包。

clan
[klæn]
名 幫派

They formed a clan of their own.
他們建立了一個屬於自己的幫派。

plan
[plæn]
名 計畫

We made plans to visit the museum and the art gallery on the same day.
我們定下計畫在同一天去參觀博物館跟美術館。

span
[spæn]
名 跨距

What is the span of the wings on that airplane?
那架飛機的翼展長度是多少？

ice
[aɪs]
名 冰

You can see the snow and ice on top of that mountain.
你可以看到那座山頂的冰雪。

navy
[ˋnevɪ]
名 海軍

My brother works in the navy.
我的哥哥在海軍服務。

omit
[oˋmɪt]
動 刪除

Omit unnecessary words in your writing.
把文章中不必要的字刪掉。

bark
[bɑrk]
名 樹皮

This tree has very thick, brown bark.
這棵樹有很厚的棕色樹皮。

bunk
[bʌŋk]
名 (上、下舖的)床舖

The children have a bunk bed in their room.
這些孩子的房間裡有一張雙層床。

clank
[klæŋk]
動 發叮噹聲

The pans fell and clanked on the floor.
這些平底鍋掉到地上叮噹作響。

plank
[plæŋk]
名 厚板

The plank down there is broken.
那邊那塊厚板子斷掉了。

spank
[spæŋk]
動 打…的屁股

She spanked her daughter for stealing the candy.
她打女兒的屁股，因為她偷糖果。

vice
[vaɪs]
名 邪惡

Many religions talk of vice and virtue.
許多宗教都會談論邪惡與美德。

navvy
[ˋnævɪ]
名 挖土工人

He's employed as a navvy.
他受雇為挖土工人。

vomit
[ˋvɑmɪt]
動 嘔吐

I have diarrhea and keep vomiting. I think it was something I ate.
我拉肚子又不停嘔吐。我想大概是吃壞肚子了。

想想看 要將填入的字改為合乎文法的形式喔！

下面這些句子少了哪個字？

bun	*span*
omit	*plank*
spank	*bark*
plan	*ice*

1. **It's expected that this _______ will solve our money problems.**
   這個計畫有希望能解決我們的金錢問題。

2. **The weather was so cold that the lake turned to _______.**
   天氣冷到湖都結冰了。

3. **She _______ the unimportant details of the story.**
   她把故事中不重要的細節刪去。

4. **This soup is served with a _______ and butter.**
   這道湯要搭配小圓麵包和湯一起吃。

5. **She _______ her daughter for telling a lie.**
   她因為女兒撒謊揍她屁股。

6. **They used several _______ to fix the roof of their old house.**
   他們用幾塊木板修理老家的屋頂。

7. **This tree has thick, rough _______.**
   這棵樹的樹皮又厚又粗。

找找看

以下句子在前面都出現過，你確定都讀熟了嗎？
找找看下面的句子有沒有拼錯的字。
錯字訂正於上方箭頭處，沒錯字請打“○”

下面哪些句子有字拼錯了？

8 →

My brother works in the navvy.

我的哥哥在海軍服務。

9 →

The pans fell and claned on the floor.

這些平底鍋掉到地上叮噹作響。

10 →

I have diarrhea and keep omiting. I think it was something I ate.

我拉肚子又不停嘔吐。我想大概是吃壞肚子了。

11 →

This tree has very thick, brown bark.

這棵樹有很厚的棕色樹皮。

12 →

They formed a clan of their own.

他們建立了一個屬於自己的幫派。

13 →

She planked her daughter for stealing the candy.

她打女兒的屁股，因為她偷糖果。

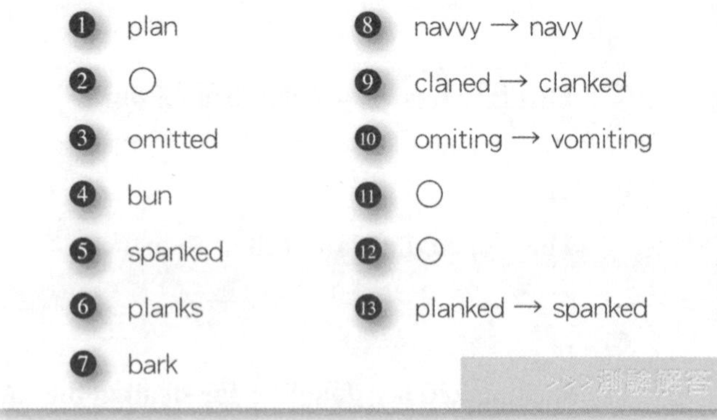

1. plan
2. ○
3. omitted
4. bun
5. spanked
6. planks
7. bark
8. navvy → navy
9. claned → clanked
10. omiting → vomiting
11. ○
12. ○
13. planked → spanked

>>>測驗解答

索引

A

B

索引

C

索引

索引

索引

索引

索引

索引

索引

國家圖書館出版品預行編目資料

單字加碼記憶法一挑戰級 ／ 吳惠珠

易說館編輯部編著. -- 初版. -- 臺北市
:日月文化, 2007. 12
240面：13 × 19 公分. --（易說館：22）
ISBN 978-986-6823-46-6 (平裝附光碟片)
1.英語 2.詞彙
805.12 96019498

易說館 22

單字加碼記憶法一挑戰級

作　　者：吳惠珠
總 編 輯：陳思容
執行編輯：趙育芳
文字編輯：漆聯榮・鄭彥谷
英文主筆：Mark Hammous・Craig Borowski・Jennfer Johnston・Thomas Walk
中文翻譯：林雅玲
英文錄音：Kronis Kent Krahn・Stephanie Hong
Debra Thoreson
校　　對：吳惠珠・林雅玲
美術設計：許家銘

董 事 長：洪祺祥
發 行 人：張水江
總 經 理：蕭豔秋
行銷總監：蔡雍
法律顧問：孫隆賢
財務顧問：蕭聰傑

出　　版：日月文化出版股份有限公司
發　　行：日月文化出版股份有限公司
地　　址：台北市信義路三段151號9樓
電　　話：(02) 2708-5509
傳　　真：(02) 2708-6157
E-mail　：service@heliopolis.com.tw
郵撥帳號：19716071 日月文化出版股份有限公司

總 經 銷：大和書報圖書股份有限公司
電　　話：(02)8990-2588
傳　　真：(02)2299-7900、2290-1658
印　　刷：禹利電子分色有限公司
初　　版：2007年12月
定　　價：350元
ISBN　：978-986-6823-46-6

日月文化集團 HELIOPOLIS CULTURE GROUP

親愛的讀者您好：

感謝您購買易說館的書籍。
為提供完整服務與快速資訊，請詳細填寫下列資料，傳真至 (02) 2708-6157，或免貼郵票寄回，我們將不定期提供您新書資訊及最新優惠訊息。

易說館 讀者服務卡

感謝您購買《單字加碼記憶法—挑戰級》敬請填寫以下問題：

*1. 讀友姓名：________________________________

*2. 身分證字號：________________________________

*3. 聯絡地址：________________________________

*4. 電子郵件信箱：________________________________

(以上欄位請務必填寫，身分證字號為您的讀友編號，僅供內部使用，日月文化保證絕不做其他用途，請放心！)

5. 您購買的書名：________________________________

6. 購自何處：__________ 縣/市 __________ 書店

7. 您的性別：□男　□女　生日：____年____月____日

8. 您的職業：□製造　□金融　□軍公教　□服務　□資訊　□傳播　□學生　□自由業　□其他

9. 您從哪裡得知本書消息？　□書店　□網路　□報紙　□雜誌　□廣播　□電視　□他人推薦　□其他

10. 您通常以何種方式購書？ □書店　□網路　□傳真訂購　□郵購劃撥　□其他

11. 您希望我們為您出版哪類書籍？　□文學　□科普　□財經　□行銷　□管理　□心理　□健康　□傳記　□小說　□休閒　□旅遊　□童書　□家庭　□其他

12. 您對本書的評價：

(請填寫代號　1.非常滿意　2.滿意　3.普通　4.不滿意　5.非常不滿意)

書名_____內容______ 封面設計______ 版面編排______文／譯筆 _______

13. 請給我們建議：

____

____

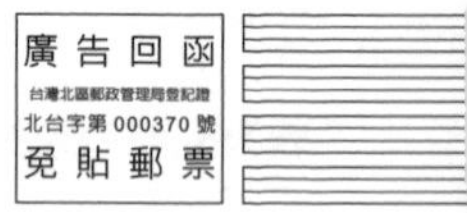

讀者服務部　收

10658　台北市信義路三段 151 號 9 樓

對折黏貼後，即可直接郵寄

日月文化集團之友長期獨享郵撥購書 75 折優惠（單筆購書金額 500 元以下請另附掛號郵資 60 元），請於劃撥單上註明身分證字號（即會員編號），以便確認。

成為日月文化集團之友的 2 個方法：

- 完整填寫書後的讀友回函卡，傳真或郵寄（免付郵資）給我們。
- 直接劃撥購書，於劃撥單通訊欄註明姓名、地址、電子郵件信箱、身分證字號以便建檔。

劃撥帳號：19716071　　戶名：日月文化出版股份有限公司
讀者服務電話：(02)2708-5509　讀者服務傳真：(02) 2708-6157
客服信箱：service@heliopolis.com.tw

大好書屋

寶鼎出版

唐莊文化

山岳文化

易說館